THE QUESTION

OUR SOUL NEVER DIES; ITS JOURNEY JUST BEGINS.

NAIRB'S STORIES BOOK TWO

GREG SIOFER

CONTENTS

THANK YOU

I would like to thank my loving parents, Tadeusz and Urszula Siofer and my lovely daughter Isabella Siofer.

CHAPTER 1: THE CABIN

My chest pounds as I stare ahead. I glue my eyes to the moving dust of the illumination ray as I wait. I step forward slowly, taking a deep breath.

"Grace," I whisper.

I scan the bright room; I notice something on the floor a few meters away. As I pick it up, observing it as I turn it, my eyes widen, and I realize it's the same Hugo Victor rose I gave Grace.

"Grace!" I say louder, standing up.

"Grace," I repeat, my eyes moving as I wait for a reply.

The cabin is silent. I look down to see a drop of my tear on the floor in a blur, just listening to the wind. "There is no reply; the cabin is silent. The only sound is the wind blowing outside its walls.

"Grace, I need you," I say softly. Still silence.

I look down at the flower I'm holding and see a drop of my tear splashing across the floor as one of the petals fall off.

"Grace," I call out.

I walk to the couch. With moist eyes, I place the rose on the coffee table beside it, then sit down, cover my face with my hands, and weep for a few moments. Then, grief turning to confusion, I lay down, resting my head on my forearm at the end of the couch. I turn my gaze to the window, where I see trees moving from side to side, then close my eyes and listen to the wind hitting the cabin. I hear a knock, and when I open my eyes, it's calm outside, and the trees are still through the window.

The knock gets louder. "I'm coming," I yell, walking to the door.

Opening it, I find Jim standing there, holding a bag.

"You look like you have a hangover," he says.

"Come in," I reply, opening the door.

"I have good news to share. I spoke to your parents, calmed them down, and picked up breakfast for you," Jim says.

Approaching me, he hands me the plastic bag. "Thank you," I say, placing it on the coffee table.

"Come sit down. I want to show you something," I say, nodding toward the couch.

Picking up the rose, I sit down beside Jim.

"Does this look familiar to you?" I ask.

After looking at it intently for a few moments, Jim says, "Yes, isn't it similar to the rose I gave you?"

"No, it is not similar. It's the same rose. It even has my nail mark on it," I say, pointing.

"Really?" His eyes widen. "Well, where did you get this rose from?"

"It got dark for a few minutes when I was lying on the couch last night, and I got up and discovered a rose in the middle of the room on the floor."

"I need to sit down."

"You are sitting."

"That's right, I am."

We sit in silence for a minute.

"Why is there broken glass here on the floor?" Jim asks.

Looking at my cut, I respond, "I tried to hit the fly."

After my cut disappears, I go and pick up the glass, place it on the coffee table, then sit back down beside him.

"Grace is monitoring you, I think," Jim says, staring at me.

"You think?"

"I cannot explain it in any other way."

I gaze into Jim's eyes momentarily, my thoughts becoming empty.

"Watch my finger," I tell him.

I cut my finger with the shard of glass, then observe the wound quickly fading.

"Nairb, you've shown me this before."

I reach for the brandy bottle underneath the coffee table and then take a few sips.

"You're right, but look now."

Once again, I cut my finger, and as we watch, the incision remains.

"It is not disappearing," Jim says.

I reach for a tissue from the box on the coffee table to stop the bleeding.

"After the alcohol has gone from my body, it will."

Patting the cut with the tissue, I put my finger in my mouth and then out again.

"You don't have your powers anymore?" Jim inquires.

"Let me try something that I attempted last night," I say, turning to gaze at the fireplace. "Nothing happened when I looked at the wood in the fireplace. It's all powers that I got. I just tried to start a fire."

"I think I know why I couldn't save Grace," I say, glancing at Jim, my eyes getting moist. "I had a few glasses of wine."

Jim places his hand on my shoulder and looks into my eyes.

"Don't blame yourself. There is no way you could have known."

After a few seconds pass, I say, "You are right. I wish I had been able to save her."

Standing up, I grab the bag of food Jim brought, and start walking toward the kitchen.

"Hey, where is Dawna?"

"Connie picked her up, and they went shopping at that mall I met her at to get you some things. They will come here when they are done."

"Okay, sounds good. Do you want anything while I'm in here?"

"Actually, yes, can you grab me the bag of chips in that upper cabinet," Jim asked as he pointed to the cabinet.

"This one?" I asked.

"Yes, just grab the whole bag," Jim replies.

I open the cabinet and take the blue plastic bag of chips.

I turn and walk towards Jim and sit beside him, passing him the bag of chips.

As Jim took the chip bag, he grabbed a few chips, stood up and placed the chip bag on the coffee table before walking towards the window.

"The whole situation is a mess, but don't worry. We'll get through it," he said as he placed a few chips in his mouth. "Lets watch some TV for now," we walked over to the couch and sat.

We hear a knock.

"That must be the girls," I say, walking to the door and opening it.

Dawna steps inside, then Connie, holding a blue bag. I close the door behind them.

"Hi, Nairb."

"Good morning, Dawna. Hi, Connie."

The girls follow me to the living room. Connie and I sit beside Jim on the couch, while Dawna flops down on the loveseat.

"How are you doing?" Connie asks. "Dawna explained everything to me."

"I'm okay, but I'm a little lost."

"Don't worry; we've got you covered," she says, patting my leg.

Connie digs into the shopping blue bag and pulls out a blue pair of jeans and a white sweater. "What do you think?"

I clutch the sweater, then grab the jeans. "I like them. I'll go try these on."

As I begin to walk away, I look out the window and notice a police cruiser driving slowly by.

In a panicked voice, I yell, "Jim!"

"What?"

"Look," I say, pointing at the window.

Coming over to me, his eyes follow my finger, and his eyes widen. "We need to go. Follow me."

I get behind Jim, happy to let him lead.

I follow Jim over to the fireplace, where he stops, reaching his hand out to touch the corner of the painting that is hanging on the wall beside my head.

A black door-shaped opening appears beside the fireplace.

"Let's go." Jim pats my right shoulder and walks through the entrance. My mouth gaped open in awe.

CHAPTER 2: ENTRANCE

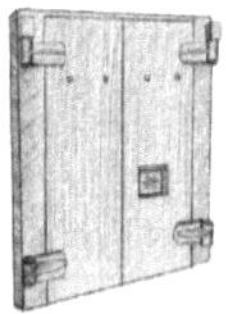

I follow Jim just inside the entranceway. He stops and presses a red button on the wall, turning on a light.

As the door closes, the illumination shows us a long, narrow tunnel.

Jim pats my right shoulder and says, "Let's go."

What I just witnessed makes me hesitate momentarily, but remembering the police back where we came from, I start walking toward Jim.

"I didn't know there was a secret entrance there. Why didn't you tell me?"

"You didn't ask."

"So next time, I should ask if there is a secret escape route from here?"

In response to my question, Jim smiles.

"Is this tunnel something that's been here for a long time?"

"Remember how I said I got the cabin from my parents? Who got it from theirs?"

"Yes."

"Well, my grandfather was a secret agent, and he was always fearful that someone was after him. He built this tunnel and prepared a hideout, where we are going now."

"I see. Wait. What about Dawna and Connie?"

"Don't worry. Dawna knows the plan. We will meet later."

"Okay."

I wonder why he didn't tell me about this plan earlier. After walking for several minutes, we come to a dead end.

"Here we go," Jim says, pressing a button.

I hear the faint sound of birds as another entranceway opens, a bright light shining through it.

Jim glances at me briefly, then walks into the light; I follow him.

We proceed into the middle of the forest where Grace and I used to wander.

"I didn't know this was here."

"That's the whole point. Nobody knows. It is a promise I made to my parents, and it is a promise they made to theirs. Only in emergencies does it come into play," Jim explains as he lifts a rock and presses another button.

"Follow me. I'll show you the bunker."

The two of us walk through the trees for a few minutes, until a loud howl breaks the silence.

Jim puts his hand on my chest and says, "Don't move."

I glance up and see a pack of coyotes. We watch them cross in front of us, the last one turning its head in our direction. After looking into each other's eyes for a few seconds, the coyote grunts, then barks, before leaping at us with the rest of the pack.

"Nairb, now would be a good time to set a tree on fire in their direction," Jim says in a panicked tone.

"I am trying! To start a fire."

"It's not working, Jim."

"What do you mean it isn't working?"

"It's not working!" I shout, looking at him.

A dazzling white light figure appears in front of us, almost blinding us.

Jim slaps my chest and says, "Run, Nairb, think about it later."

We both turn around and start sprinting through the forest.

"Get up there quickly," Jim says, pointing at a tall tree.

Stopping in front of it, we clamber up, Jim first, with me right behind him, hearing the coyotes yelping. My right leg feels like it's stuck on something when I try to lift it, and when I look down, I see a coyote holding on to my bottom pant leg with its teeth.

"Get off!" I shout, moving my leg from side to side, kicking at the wild animal.

It loses its grip and falls on its back. Quickly getting up, the rest of the pack join it, looking up and pacing around.

I climb higher and sit beside Jim on a branch.

"You alright?" he asks.

Looking down at my ripped jeans, I reply, "Yes, I'm fine."

"That was close. We'll be here for a while."

"Yes, I think so," I reply, glancing down at the coyotes.

"Make yourself comfortable. Why didn't you use your fire?"

"I don't know. I tried, and it didn't work."

"Strange."

"Jim, it's gone."

"What is?"

"My ability to start a fire is gone."

"Are you serious?"

"Yes, I keep trying, but nothing happens."

"Your fire stopped working at the best time. Thank God for the bright light. It allowed us to flee on time."

"Yes, I was wondering what that white figure was?"

"Let's not worry about it right now. We must figure out how to get down."

"We'll wait until they lose interest. Do you remember the lake we were stuck on for a while?"

#

"Yes, Mom. Jim and I are taking the boat to the lake."

"Okay, just keep your distance."

"I'll do that."

After reaching the boat, I get inside while Jim pushes it and jumps in. He grabs the motor's handle and sits on the bench, pulling the line to turn it on. "Here we go," I say as we slowly pass my mom, sitting in a beach chair, waving back at us as the boat moves away. The wind hits my face as Jim speeds up. My right hand touches the water as the boat bounces around, and the waves splash my face gently.

"We are almost in the middle of the lake," Jim announces loudly.

He cuts the engine, and we cease moving.

"Why did you stop?" I ask, looking at him.

"It just turned off; let me turn it back on," Jim says, pulling the rusty reddish wire.

Pulling the line a few times, his face turns red. "Nairb, we have a problem."

"What's wrong?" I ask.

"The motor is not starting," Jim replies, sitting back down on the dump bench.

"What do you mean it won't turn on?" I inquire in a louder voice.

"It won't turn on. Oh, hey, did you eat?"

"Yes, before we got to the boat. Why do you ask?"

"We are going to be here a while," Jim says, looking at me.

I lean against the side wall of the boat.

"What do you mean, a while?"

"We won't move, so we'll have to wait until someone comes by."

I put my legs up on a bench in front of me and lean back, touching the inside of the boat's front wood walls. The water gently rocks the boat up and down as I look from side to side, yawning as I close my eyes.

After hearing a strange sound, I immediately open my eyes and see a large green boat.

I get up and scream while waving, "Over here!"

Then I yell loudly to Jim to get up.

"What?" Jim rubs his eyes.

"There is a boat. Get up!"

Jim turns his head to the right, then stands up, and we both scream and wave.

Finally, we see the boat turn its direction toward us.

"I remember being in that boat for a few hours. It's good your mom wondered why we were gone for so long."

"Lucky us," I say.

Seeing the coyotes still pacing in circles, I lean against a thick branch.

"Nairb, why don't you move the time forward for a few hours? They should be gone by then."

"Okay, what time do you have?"

"Twelve."

No matter how hard I concentrate on the tree, nothing happens.

"Are you doing it? There is a coyote looking at me, showing its teeth."

"Yes, just hold on a sec. I'm having technical difficulties."

"Whenever you're ready."

A few moments pass by.

"Did you do it?" Jim asks, looking down. "I still see them, Nairb."

"Well, Jim, I guess we'll be stuck here for a while."

I readjust myself after slipping down in the tree a bit.

"Are you okay?"

I lift my foot back up and say, "Yes, I'm fine, but my time forward is not working."

"It's not working either?"

"That's what I said, Jim; it's not working," I reply loudly.

"Can you fix it?"

"I don't know how."

There is silence, as we know what is at stake. Jim's expression shows that he is scared, but he says nothing.

During our conversation, Grace's voice echoed in my head as we reflected on the good old days.

"Nairb, the coyotes have gone," Jim exclaims, breaking the silence.

I look down. "They're gone!"

I follow Jim as he descends slowly. Looking around, I ensure they are all gone before we put our feet on the ground.

"Let's go," he says, patting my arm.

"Thank you so much, Jim, for your help."

"No problem, Nairb. I'm sure you'd do the same," Jim says with a smile.

As we walk, I realize how colorful the trees are.

After a minute, Jim says we have reached our destination.

"Where? All I see are trees and shrubs."

"See those two trees that are touching?" he says, pointing at them.

"Yes, what about them?"

"There is a rock covering a black button behind them. Come on, let's go!"

A shout rings out as Jim runs toward the tree, me following him.

"Now watch," Jim says as we approach the tree. He lifts a rock covered in green moss and presses a black button.

There is a loud sound. As I turn my head toward the noise, my eyes widen.

CHAPTER 3: INSIDE

The rocky hill across from us appears to have another black door-shape opening, moving up and to the right, as if in a movie.

"It just looked like a hill of rocks."

"Looks can be deceiving," Jim says.

"I never imagined there would be an entrance there. It looks so naturally hidden there."

"That's the whole point, right? Come on, let's go!"

Upon approaching the black entrance, goosebumps form on my arms as I hear air being drawn in like a magnet. We enter, and we are surrounded by darkness.

As the door closes behind us, rocks grind against one another as Jim flicks the switch, bringing the lights on revealing a tunnel.

A red steel door appears after we walk a few feet.

Jim grasps the handle and opens it.

As we walk through, into a small room, the door closes behind me. In the corner is a bed, a sofa close by, with a small coffee table in front of it, gray wooden shelves with various items, and a small white fridge. This area has a stale smell. Jim takes a seat on the sofa, and I follow him. I fix my eyes on a black wire that is holding a light bulb from the ceiling.

"What do you think?"

"I like it," I say.

"You will be safe here, and that door is your emergency exit." Jim points behind the sofa to a white steel door.

As Jim stands up, he walks over to the shelves, picks up a brown box, blows dust off it, and leaves a grayish cloud behind.

He places the box on the coffee table, that has legs that look like they might buckle at any moment, and wipes the remaining dust off before he opens the box. Grabbing a white square, he pulls it up as he stands.

"It looks like a television, Jim."

He pulls it out of the box and places it on the table. "I wonder if it still works?"

Throwing the box aside, he removes the antennas from the back. After adjusting them to see if he can receive a signal, Jim hits the "On" switch.

"Look, I'm on TV!" Jim exclaims, once the picture comes into view.

It is suspected that Jim is assisting Nairb in his crimes. If you see him, don't approach him; instead, contact the police immediately.

"Look at us; we're famous," Jim says.

"Do me a favor and turn off the television."

Walking up to the set, Jim picks it up, looking red. Swinging his hands to the right, he releases the television, which shatters against the brick wall. A loud bang causes a small crack in the wall, and the rest of it falls to the floor.

"There, no turning off required," Jim says, looking at me.

As a droplet runs down his face, I stay silent and let Jim have his moment. After a minute, he stands up straight.

"Jim, your right hand has a cut."

He looks down. "So it does. I'm fine."

I pat the sofa. "No, you're not! Sit beside me; maybe I'll fix it."

Jim sits down beside me, and I grasp his hand.

"Look! It disappeared. I think I still have it."

"Great!" Jim pulls his hand away. "Tomorrow, I will introduce you to Patty. She can help us."

Jim walks toward the shelves and picks up two dusty old cell phones, gently throwing one at me. "I'm sure you want to speak with your parents. You have thirty seconds, then hang up, as their phone is most likely monitored."

"Thanks, Jim. How do you know all this?"

"Many things I know from Patty. Hence, these phones are from her."

As I flip open the phone, I touch the number pad with my shaky finger. Placing the receiver to my right ear, I hear it ringing.

"Hello."

"Mom."

"Nairb, are you alright?"

"Everything is fine, Mom."

"The police are searching for you and Jim, and you both appeared on television."

"Don't worry, Mom, I know. I'm sorry, but I'm short on time." The background noise intensifies with a rapid thumping sound.

"Do you need anything?"

"I'm okay. I just called you guys to let you know that everything is okay. I love you."

Just as I am about to hang up, my mom's voice breaks into tears and she says, "We love you, son."

"Don't worry, Nairb, you'll get to see them again." I glance at Jim with glossy eyes as he pats my back. Taking the cell phone, he separates the battery and places it on the table.

"It's my turn to make a call, to Patty," Jim says, dialing, then hitting the speaker button and holding the phone out.

After a few rings, she answers.

"20, 20," Patty says.

"10, 10," Jim replies.

"Yes, 60, 79."

"40, 40."

"63,64."

"98, 98."

Jim hangs up and looks at me. "We are all set for this evening."

"Well, that was strange. You guys just spoke numbers."

"Our phone conversation might be monitored, so instead of words, we use number codes. 10, 10 means it is clear to come over. 98, 98 means okay; we will come this evening." Jim takes out the batteries and places them on the table.

"Interesting."

"Don't worry. You will learn it. Come, let's meet up with Dawna and Connie."

Rising from the sofa and pulling on the wire to turn off the light bulb, we slowly make our way toward the red steel door.

Grasping the handle and opening it, I enter the pitch-black room, Jim following closely behind. As we take a few steps, Jim rushes forward and presses a button, causing me to hear grinding. As the opening widens, light rays become brighter. Placing my right hand in front of my eyes, I turn my head and gaze at Jim.

"Let's go." Jim leads the way toward the light as I trail behind him.

As we enter the light, hands shading our eyes, the trees and surrounding forest slowly come into view. Quickly, Jim runs behind the tree we had entered, lifts the rock, presses the button, and the entrance starts to close.

Jim approaches me, taps my arm, and says, "Come on," and then leads as I follow.

We walk for a few minutes, until Jim spots Dawna and dashes toward her.

I see a brown, dry, and cracked maple leaf falling behind Jim as he runs. When I double-turn my eyes, I glue them on it as it falls behind him. As everything else fades away, the falling leaf remains prominent. While observing the leaf, I notice police officers hiding behind the trees, their small black guns pointed toward the ground.

"Jim, wait!" I exclaim.

The police emerge from hiding, eliciting a scream from me.

I hear a piercing sound, then someone shouting, "Cease fire!" in the background.

With wide, glossy eyes, Jim turns his head to look at me and drops to the ground, his knees hitting first.

CHAPTER 4: JIM

My body heats instantly as I bolt toward Jim, yelling, "Noooo," and dashing left and right at full speed, dodging trees. I fall to my knees in front of him, and he looks asleep.

As Dawna stands frozen, I glance at her. "What have you done?" I ask, looking back at Jim.

As my gaze moves downward, I observe an intense dark red color surrounding the hole in his shirt near his midsection. I take hold of his weightless right arm, and as I do, I feel my energy draining away while watching his hand start moving. With each passing moment, my grip grows tighter, my knuckles turn white, and the drainage grows more intense. My midsection sinks onto Jim's stomach as I look at him and see his eyes opening, feeling powerless to stop it, and my vision blurs as his glossy eyes reflect me.

I feel his hands on my shoulders as he sits up and screams for me to stay with him. A bright figure appears before us, emitting a bright light that forces the officers and Dawna to turn their heads away from it.

Jim looks twice. "Quickly, head toward that crack that shows the bunker. Get up!" Jim helps me up as I feel weightless." Jim says loudly.

Upon entering, I glance over and observe everyone by the trees, shielding their eyes from the bright light emanating from the figure. The figure disappears when the crack starts to close, and the officers rush toward us as it fully shuts.

"Take a rest on the sofa," Jim instructs, removing his arm from my neck as I fall onto the sofa.

When I open my eyes, I see Jim sitting on a chair by the sofa, and I am lying under a blue blanket. Gripping the fabric, I push it down as I sit up.

I look at Jim. "Have I been out long?"

Jim leaves the chair and starts moving toward me.

"A day?" I say sarcastically.

"Yes, a day. You were completely out."

"How did you do that?"

"Do what?"

"That crack was a portal to here."

"I don't know. I was thinking of this bunker."

"It doesn't matter. We are safe."

"I'm sorry about Dawna."

With watery eyes, Jim sits beside me.

"Yes, me too; I'm really confused as to why she would do that. It's not like her."

"Don't worry, I'm sure there was a good reason," I say, tapping his back.

"Yes, you are right."

"Does Dawna know about this place?"

"No, she does not. We are safe here."

Just as we are talking, the phone on the table rings and the room dims, capturing our attention.

"There's no battery in that phone, Nairb!" We give each other a startled look. "Don't just sit there; pick it up and answer it."

My hand shakes as I reach for the black cell phone. I turn to look at Jim and then back to the phone before picking it up. I flip it open, then put the phone against my ear.

"Hello," I say softly.

From the corner of my eye, I see Jim gazing at me as I speak.

I can barely hear the person on the other end because of static, but a woman's voice whispers, "Think of a place."

"What do you mean think of a place?" I ask, but there is just silence as the connection breaks.

"Hello, hello," I bring the phone down and tap it with my other hand. "Hello, hello." I close the phone's flap and return it to the table.

"So, who was it?" Jim asks, with a serious look.

"It was hard to hear because of the static, but someone said to think of a place."

"Think of a place. That's weird."

"I tried to find out what she meant, but the call was cut off."

"Strange, but why don't you think of a place?"

"Like where?"

"Well, where did you first see Grace?"

"That flower shop close to my parent's house."

"Okay, why don't you think about that, then?"

"This absolutely makes no sense, but it's worth a try."

My eyes grow blurry as I remember the flower shop where I first saw Grace.

"Look, Nairb, a crack is forming; keep thinking."

Seeing her, my heart pounds faster and louder against my chest. In my mind, I play out the moment of gazing upon the true beauty before me. I ask her for coffee and see myself blushing, palms moist from nervousness.

"Nairb, I see the cash register."

I stop paying attention and feel tears in my eyes. An enormous crack in front of me provides a view into the inside of the flower shop as if it is a window to the other room. The sound of a buzzing bee accompanies the soft glow it emits. I walk toward it and lift my hand in front of it.

"What are you doing?" Jim asks, intrigued.

"I need to try something," I say, looking at my hand.

I punch my hand into the crack, feeling nothing. I look at Jim, close my eyes, and step forward, finding myself at the flower shop. As I turn my head and open my eyes, I see a hole in the wall emitting a gentle glow of light at the edges. The flower shop is illuminated, and I see Jim at the bunker, with a light reflecting on his face. He is looking right at me, but he is in the bunker.

"Are you alright?" Jim asks.

"Yes, I'm fine. They seem to be closed, and now the lights are off. Step inside."

I look forward, moving slowly, step by step, my eyes scanning the area.

"This is baffling, Nairb," he says, following me

I quickly glance back and see the glowing crack in the bunker behind us.

"I think we are here alone," I tell him.

"Yes, I think so; it's very silent. We should go back."

"Yes, you're right. Let's go back into the gap before our bunker disappears."

"You think it will do that?"

"I think so. I saw movies that this resembles, and their portal closes after a few minutes."

"Nairb, the crack is shrinking. Hurry!"

I trail behind Jim as he quickly makes his way to the crack. We step through it and arrive at the bunker. I watch as the crack shrinks, taking with it the image of the flower shop. Without a sound, the crack vanishes, and the bright light that has been brightening the area disappears.

Jim walks to the sofa and sits down, and I follow behind him.

"Well, that was interesting," I say.

"Interesting? This is unbelievable, Nairb. Do you know what this means?"

"That we can go places?" I respond.

"Yes, and you're not excited about that?"

"I am."

"Well, you sure don't look like you are."

"I am. Just a lot of things are on my mind, and I don't know how to approach this," I say, looking deeply into Jim's eyes.

"Don't worry. What's on your mind?"

"I tried to talk to Grace about it, but I was very confused and brushed it off."

"Go on," Jim says, his eyes full of interest.

"I had a dream where I saw how she was going to die and what just happened. I saw Dawna's betrayal, you getting shot by the cops, and even glimpses of my kid. I was very confused and woke up totally wet, with a scar that sometimes appears, but all those events are coming true. I'm not concerned about the police, as something more powerful will come after us. Even if we're surrounded by the police, they will be powerless and crumble before it."

"Something? Who is something?"

"I'm not sure. I woke up just as I lifted my head." I reply.

"This is deep, Nairb."

"I know. I stayed quiet because I thought it was a dream. But then everything started happening exactly like I saw it."

Jim is quiet as a mouse and looks pale.

"Let's not worry about it now. There are places I want to go." Jim gives my leg a pat.

"I thought you were more upset about Dawna?"

"I'm disappointed, but I won't make the same mistake of jumping to conclusions again. Eventually, I will talk with her, but right now, your safety is my key priority," Jim says, rubbing his thumbs together.

"I hear what you're saying." I say.

"Do you recall that hill with the view over Hamilton?" Jim asks.

"The one where we went camping with your parents?"

"It's private and won't be visible."

I begin to concentrate and envision myself running around with Jim on that hill.

"Narib, it's happening. I can see the grass."

I can also see the grass and the hill ending, seeing the city below through the crack as I stop imagining it in my head.

"Lead the way, Jim."

We make our way toward the crack. Jim walks through it and stands on the grass, glancing at me as I watch. With a wave of his hand, Jim turns around.

"Nairb, let's go."

As I take a deep breath, I walk through it as if it were an open door. When I look back, I see the bunker and then look at Jim again.

"Nairb, this is great."

Walking toward me, Jim squats down and rips out a handful of grass.

Some of the grass fall as he raises his hand. "Do you smell that?" he asks, looking at me.

"That grass has a brown color," I reply, looking at the grass in his hand.

Jim rapidly releases it. He rubs his hands together, "Never mind," he says, turning around. "Breathe deep, Nairb," he announces, his arms open wide.

"I see a garbage dumping site over there," I tell him, pointing to it.

Jim looks in the direction of my finger, then turning back and seeing the bunker, he says, "We should just go back."

I follow Jim, and we make it to the bunker, sit on the sofa, and observe the city below the hill as the crack closes.

"I propose we go to Connie's," I say.

"Why is that?"

"We've got to find out what went down and why Dawna did that."

"Yeah, you're right. Alright, let's head over to her," Jim answers hesitatingly.

I fixate on the view of Connie's backyard, and the image becomes visible through the crack.

"Are you sure this is correct? Flowers and grass are in my sight."

"Yes, I'm sure. Just walk through. I'll be right behind you."

We walk through the crack and onto the grass together.

When I rush to stand next to Jim, I see him sneezing.

"That freshly cut grass smells amazing," I announce.

Jim looks to his right and sees the colorful flowers.

"You sure this is right?" Jim casts a glance around.

"Yeah, we're in her backyard. I don't remember what the inside of the house looks like. C'mon, follow me."

We stroll from the lawn to her light brown wooden terrace, walk down the steps, halt at the blue wooden entrance, and knock.

Connie's soft voice calls out, "I'm coming."

As she opens the door, her eyes widen.

CHAPTER 5: CONNIE

Pulling us inside, she shuts the door and examines us, her eyes moving left to right.

"What are you guys doing here? You're nuts! The cops are searching all over for you. I'm even being watched in case you pop up."

"We want to find out what happened at the cabin and if you are okay," I say.

"Follow me, but avoid the windows."

We stroll through the narrow hallway toward a green-tiled staircase. Once we reach the top, she tells us to sit on the couch.

"I'll get some snacks," she says, turning around and swinging her ponytail.

The room has no sunlight, and the air is dry. Sitting on the yellow leather couch, Jim and I exchange glances, widen our eyes, then face forward in silence, waiting for Connie.

"I'm coming," we hear softly.

Connie is carrying a tray filled with three mugs, a teapot, milk, sugar, cookies, a cake, plates, and utensils. She sets the tray down on the coffee table, then takes a seat in a black leather chair across from us. After pouring tea into the mugs, she puts the pot down and leans back.

"Help yourselves," she says.

"We are curious about what went down after we vanished from the cabin and what happened to Dawna? Why did she turn against us?" I inquire, looking into her eyes and pouring milk into my tea.

"Once you left, Dawna went and talked to the police. I saw her chatting with someone outside," she explains, glancing at Jim.

"Go on," I say.

"Then she headed toward the door with someone; she said you guys were just here, and she showed them the path."

Leaning toward the coffee table, Jim picks up his mug of tea, swings his arm to the right, throws it, watches it shatter against the wall, and then leans back on the couch. Connie's eyes meet mine in a brief, silent exchange, and hers widen slightly.

"Sorry, Jim," Connie says, looking at him.

"It's okay. It's not your fault," he answers softly, raising his head and then slowly lowering it.

"Two officers barged into the cabin, and one of them questioned me about you, to which I denied everything."

"And then what?" I ask picking up my mug and take a gulp.

"While getting escorted out by the police, I saw

Dawna, and she just shrugged her shoulders at me. I got in my car and drove off, but I think someone's watching me. That's why I said to stay away from the windows."

"Thanks, Connie," I say, placing the cup on the table.

"Help yourselves, guys," Connie tells us.

"I'm not hungry," Jim mumbles.

Leaning toward the coffee table, I slide a piece of cake on a plate with a fork. Then, I lean back on the couch, holding the plate on my lap.

As I take a bite, I feel something warm on my leg.

"Bad dog, Sniffles!" Connie shouts. She sprints toward the dog and snatches her up. "Nairb, I'm so sorry."

"She likes you," Jim remarks, laughing.

Casting a quick glance at Jim, I reassure Connie that it's fine as I put my plate down on the table.

Connie looks down and says, "Let me get a cloth."

As Connie heads toward the kitchen, I notice my wet pant leg, and then I shift my gaze to Jim, who is laughing. She comes back with a cloth in her hand, stops, and squats down beside my leg.

"What is so funny?"

"Nothing," Jim replies, looking at me, answering with a chuckle.

After wiping my right pant leg, Connie exclaims, "There, that should fix it," looking red.

"Don't worry about it."

Connie glances at me for a moment before heading back to the kitchen. I glance at my right pant leg, noticing the bottom is darker, where it is wet.

I hear the water tap in the kitchen being turned on

and off a few seconds later. Then Connie comes back into the room and sits down on the chair across from us.

Connie apologizes again.

"We just got Sniffles, and she's being trained," she says, pouring tea into her cup.

"Did Dawna seem normal, or was something different?" Jim asks Connie.

"She didn't show any emotion, and she acted differently, almost like she was someone else," Connie told him.

Jim and I briefly lock eyes, and he says, "That's strange. Why'd she do that, I wonder?"

"How did you guys get here, anyway?" Connie asks, changing the subject.

"Nairb can go to places if he pictures them."

"Really?"

Jim looks at me, "Show her."

I picture the beach where Grace built her sandcastle.

#

"I can't keep my feet on the ground when I walk, Nairb."

I squint my eyes and look down. "You're right, but we're practically at the shore," I say, pointing to the pristine blue water.

As Grace enters the lake, she creates splashes. With her hands twirling the water, she says, "Come, Nairb, the water is warm," showing a red color.

I dash forward from the sand, creating splashes as I leap toward her, causing her to turn her head.

I glance at Grace, with my red eyes as my hands slide back across my head.

"You were right; the water's warm." I turn toward her as I feel the wetness streaming down my face.

As I slap the water with my open hands, Grace turns away from me, and I come to a halt. Then she looks at me and does the same as I did, and I quickly turn away before the water can hit me in the face.

"Alright, you win!" she exclaims, water dripping from her hair.

"Let's get out," she says, turning, creating a swirl on the surface.

With every step, I feel the warmth of the sand on my feet. I watch Grace's blue swimsuit blend with the water as I walk behind her, using my open hands to move the water through my fingers. My hands turn light red as I look down.

Grace sprints toward the shoreline as the water calmly spills onto it and then retreats. She lifts her hand and waves at me before sitting on the dark yellow sand.

"Nairb, come sit beside me. We're going to build a sandcastle." Using both her hands, she begins to collect some.

Sitting next to her, I observe the water gently touching my lower feet, creating a light redness that spreads up my body.

"Start digging over there," Grace points with enthusiasm.

While digging alongside her, a gentle warmth spreads through my body.

"Hey, are you there, Nairb?" Jim gently pats my back.

"Oops, sorry, I was lost in thought," I reply, looking at Jim with a glazed expression.

"You had us worried, looking all frozen like that."

I glance at Connie briefly and then say, "I'm good. Here you go."

A few meters in front of us, a crack appears, and the beach picture becomes wider and clearer with each passing second.

The light reflects off of Connie as she nears the entryway, and her eyes are fixed on it with complete concentration. Her hand touches the view of the sandy beach, and as she gradually pulls back her finger, the inside of the crack springs back to its original location.

With a humming sound coming from it, she excitedly says, "I can see the beach!"

"Walk through it. We'll be right behind you."

Connie closes her eyes before stepping forward into the crack; Jim and I follow.

"Nairb, this is incredible," Connie exclaims.

"Sure is," Jim says.

"Nairb? You, okay?" Connie inquires.

I turn to her and say, "Sorry, I'm fine. It's just that Grace and I built a sandcastle here," I reply, my eyes moist.

Connie embraces me tightly before stepping back and gazing into my watery eyes. "I'm sure she's with you," she reassures me.

"Hey, how long will this stay this open?" Connie asks, looking at the crack.

"Only a few minutes. We should head back."

"Yes, you're right."

Glancing over Connie's shoulder, I notice Jim in his boxers and ask him what he is doing.

"I thought we were going to jump in?"

"Nope, hurry and get dressed; we're going," I tell him, then look back at Connie.

"Okay," he says softly, collecting his clothes.

They both follow me through the crack, where Jim and I make our way to the couch, and Connie takes her place in the chair. The glowing crack gradually diminishes until it vanishes completely.

Putting on his shirt, Jim turns to Connie and asks, "So, what do you think?"

With her pupils scanning left to right, she declares, "This was amazing. Just think of all the places you can see."

"I've been wanting to go back to some places for ages but never had the time. Now I do," I say, giving them a quick look.

"Let's go see them now," Jim throws on his pants and starts walking.

"Wait, weren't we going to visit Patty?" I follow Jim's movements with my head.

"We are, later on," Jim walks forward.

"Not there!" Connie yells.

"Huh? What do you mean?" Jim looks around.

"The window," Connie shouts.

Jim's body freezes for a few seconds, and his eyes widen as he looks outside. "Nairb, we have to leave now," he yells, looking down at me. Waving his fingers toward himself a few times, he signals.

"Why?"

"Time to go! Get up!" he shouts. "Quick, follow me."

I dash down the stairs with him, and we take a left.

We hear a loud crash at the main door, followed by a scream.

Connie yells, "Hurry!"

"Nairb, quick, the bunker."

The bunker image materializes in the crack.

"Hurry up and get in!" Jim shouts.

I hear someone rushing.

"Go through it now."

I do, and then I turn around and see Jim, just as a man comes into view from the corner.

"Jim, there's someone behind you," I scream.

As Jim turns around, my eyes widen.

CHAPTER 6: BEHIND

Jim sprints toward the man and leaps at his midsection, wrapping his arms around him and bringing them both to the ground.

"Jim," I scream as they roll around on the ground.

Jim punches him in the face, lifts his hand back, looks at it, shakes it like a bug was on it, then rises to his feet, just as Connie comes into sight. The man seizes the bottom of Jim's pant leg, stopping him in his step. Connie launches herself at him, freeing Jim's leg from the man's grip, and Jim dashes toward me. The man pushes Connie off of him and gets up and chases Jim.

"Hurry, Jim, it's closing," I scream.

Jim launches himself toward me, and I step to the side and see the man right behind him. Connie is still standing in the corner, gazing at Jim, with her hands resting on her cheeks. Jim lands in the bunker, hitting the wall with his back, causing the shelves to crash down to the floor and the pile of dust to rise.

The man lunged toward the crack, but it shut before he could make contact. I dash over to Jim by the wall, heart thumping, and move the dusty shelf.

"Jim, you, okay?" I ask.

He stands up, brushing off his pants. "I'm good."

"That was insane," I remark.

"Yes, it was," he says, placing the shelf against the wall.

"I thought you were a goner for sure. I'm amazed at how you did that."

"It just came naturally," Jim responds, glancing at me as he walks to the couch and sits down.

I sit down beside him, then looking at him with a serious expression, say, "Thank you, Jim."

"Don't worry about it."

"You're bleeding from your knuckle," I point out.

Jim looks down at his right hand. "It's nothing. I must have punched his tooth."

When I grab his arm, the wound disappeared, and I let go.

"Thanks," Jim says, lifting his hand and putting his knuckle toward his lips.

As we sit silently for a moment, the hanging bulb suddenly illuminates the room red. We turn our heads to look at it.

We hear banging coming from behind the red steel door.

"What is that?" I ask.

"Quick, think of the beach. We must go now," Jim yells.

"What?"

"Now, Nairb, the beach!"

A crack appears, illuminating the dark red walls and exposing the beach beyond.

"Go through now!"

I stand up, then quickly dash through, feeling the refreshing breeze on my face. Jim follows me, and then we both look back and observe the red steel door for a minute; it slams into the wall, and officers flood in, turning their heads and rushing toward us. As I sense a drop trickling down my back, I moved back a step.

"Jim."

He steps back slowly, "Quick, think of the hill."

"What hill?"

"The one earlier!"

I focus intently on the hill and a new crack appears in front of us showing the hill. Jim and I run through it and see grass. We quickly look back and see some of the officers on the beach. They lock their eyes on us for a few seconds, then begin to charge at us.

The green bench, unchanged since our failed attempt at picking up girls in our younger years, is visible through a newly formed crack. I poke Jim with my elbow, and his head turns, noticing the bench as we dash through the crack, then step on a sidewalk.

Jim stops and looked at the bus post, moving his head as he says, "I know this place."

"Yes, you do; look, the blue bus is coming, trailing black smoke behind it," I say, pointing at it. "Get on if it stops."

The bus slows down, then stops at the bus post, opening its doors. We hop on, pay the driver, and take a seat at the back of the bus, where we notice the familiar torn green plastic seat, with foam spilling out. Hearing the engine's roar, the bus starts to move.

Our heads turn to observe the crack, and we see a black cloud of smoke around the bus stop. The officers coming through begin coughing and covering their mouths, with one bending down, placing his hands on his knees. As the bus pulls away, we wave to them.

As we look back at our seats, a faint drop splashes against the floor, and we exchange smiles. Jim rubs his arm across his forehead, and we listen to the engine roar while black smoke drifts in through the open window on the right. We squint and pull our shirts over our noses.

"No way, Jim! It actually worked." I say, looking at him.

"I had a gut feeling it would. It was like in a movie I watched."

"It's good you saw it."

"At the next bus stop, let's get off just in case."

"Okay, good idea."

Jim pulls the old yellow cable hanging loosely by the open window, and we stand up. Approaching the green, rusted doors, the bus slows down, and we exchange a few seconds of eye contact before the doors open with a creak. We descend three steps of black rubber with peeling surfaces, then step onto the dirt road, with just a crooked bus post in sight.

The sound of the engine roaring fills the air as the bus doors close. As it drives away, thick black smoke trails from its rusty exhaust pipe, and we turn our heads. As we take a few steps forward, I eagerly feel my hair lifting in the wind, but before we can go any farther, a loud noise makes us gasp. We shift our gaze and behold a massive amount of black smoke emerging from a bus in the distance.

"Glad we got out of there," I exclaim, and we turn our heads and continue walking.

"Me too."

After wandering for a few minutes, a crack appears in front of us.

"What's this?" Jim asks.

"Just go through it."

Jim glances at me for a second, then steps through the crack, me trailing behind him.

"Why is it so cold here?"

"This is our ski cottage. If you look through the window, you will see snow and mountains. We are quite remote here."

"I never knew you guys had a ski cottage. Why didn't you tell me?"

"You never asked," I reply, hugging myself.

"Well, it's cold, but it's nice."

"Why don't you get the fire started? There is everything you need over there," pointing to the fireplace.

"Wait! What are you going to do?"

"I'm going to see my folks."

"I don't think it's a good idea. The cops are bound to search for us."

"Jim, relax. I got this. I won't be too long."

"Okay, if you must."

Turning away from Jim, I picture my room, and my face reflects the light. With Jim watching, I inhale deeply, step through the crack, and feel the soft and cozy red carpet of my room beneath my feet.

Glancing around, I notice my room is just as it was when I lived there. I approach my closed wooden door and as I'm about to grasp it, the knob begins to shift. Retracting my hand, I sense a sudden rush of heat throughout my body, as if it had splashed me with hot water. My eyes are glued to the silver handle as it slowly descends, causing me to step back. The fast knocking of my heart is all I can hear as the door slowly opens, and I look up. I gulp and freeze as a person appears, gazing at me.

CHAPTER 7: ROOM

"Nairb? Is it really you?"

"Hey, it's me, Mom."

Her brown hair reflects the white light as she leaps toward me and wraps her arms around me. She finally releases me and looks up, a surprised expression on her face as she sees Jim through the crack behind me.

"Hi," Jim says, waving at her at the ski cottage.

"What are you doing here? How did you get here?" my mom inquires.

"Mom, I'm able to go places now, and I wanted to let you and Dad know that Jim and I are okay."

"I'm so glad, but the cops are searching for you, and you're all over the TV. Did you kill those officers?"

"What officers, Mom?"

"The ones in the helicopter."

"Relax, Mom, they made a safe landing."

She gazes at me, with a serious expression.

"I didn't lay a finger on any police officers, Mom!"

"I believe you," she says, her tone softening. "How are you doing?"

"We had some close encounters but, thankfully, we are okay."

"Dad isn't here right now, but I can get you something to eat if you are hungry."

"Sure, that'd be outstanding. I completely forgot."

"The police are around the house, so just wait here, and I'll bring something to you."

Mom turns around and walks away, her footsteps echoing down the stairs and then along the hardwood floors, until they suddenly stop, leaving only silence in their wake. I hear the kitchen cabinets open with a loud, squeaky sound, followed by the faint clink of plates. The sound of the utensils hitting the plate was rhythmic, almost like a beat.

I hear Mom's footsteps thumping on the hardwood again, accompanied by her cheerful humming. Seconds later, she enters the room with a tray containing two plates, cutlery, and two glasses filled with coffee.

As my mom approaches me, I see steam rising from the food.

I lower my head toward the plates, inhaling the savory smell, and thank my mom.

"Good thing the police officers are outside."

"It was just made for dinner; it's still hot," she says, nodding and handing me the tray.

I picture the ski cottage, and the crack opens. We see Jim sitting on the couch, wearing a cozy red sweater by the fireplace.

"When will I see you again?" Mom asks, turning to me, her eyes full of longing.

"I'll be in touch soon. Give Dad my regards, and I love you." I turn to the crack and walk through it.

As I do, I notice the way the light hits my mom's face in my old room, casting a warm glow on everything around her. The crack shrinks, and she waves goodbye, with glossy eyes, and then the image disappears. I stare at the emptiness for a few more seconds, feeling the weight of the silence. I take a deep breath and turn around, feeling the warmth on my skin.

Walking toward Jim, I exclaim, "Look what I got!"

His eyes light up, clearly pleased at the sight of the food. "I was getting hungry," he admits, pointing to the wooden table below the slowly rotating ceiling fan.

I set the tray down with a clatter. Jim meets me and deftly grabs a plate, and utensils, before settling into the brown wooden chair.

"How did everything go at your parents' place?" He inquires, holding a fork in his left hand.

"The police are still looking for us," I tell him, taking a plate and plopping myself down.

"Yeah, I thought so."

"So, I apparently killed those police officers in the helicopter."

"What? No way," he says, between mouthfuls. "I saw the helicopter land safely."

"That's what they're saying on TV," I reply, then take a bite.

"Don't worry, it'll clear up soon," he reassures me while spearing peas.

"Yeah, you're right."

We share our meal for a few minutes, occasionally hearing slurping and the empty swallow of air.

"That was good," Jim says, pushing his plate away.

"Mom cooked it. I'm stoked you liked it. It was one perk living there."

"Oh, I get it now. That's why you took forever to move in with Grace."

Jim's mention of Grace triggers thoughts of her in my mind.

#

"Nairb, this place is freaking amazing!" Grace exclaims, running toward the window. "Look at this view, the mountains covered in snow."

She quickly glances at me, smiling, then stokes wood in the fireplace.

"I'm glad you like it."

"Like it. It's outstanding! Look at all that snow coming down. I feel like I'm in a movie with Santa living next door, just peeking through the window."

"Would you like some hot chocolate? "

"That would be great. The walk here made me cold," she says, removing her jacket and strolling toward the brown couch.

"I'm on it," I say, opening the kitchen cabinet.

"I wasn't aware you had a remote cabin?"

"I don't usually say anything." I carry a cup over to Grace and sit down beside her.

"Here you go," I say, handing it to her.

"Thanks!" Grace takes the cup and takes a sip.

"Grace, look at me for a sec," I say.

"Sure thing," she replies, placing the cup on the table.

"I'm ready to move forward in our relationship."

"Forward. I'm confused. What do you mean?" Grace asks, her blue eyes reflecting my redness.

"I just want us to be together," I tell her, feeling warmth spreading inside me.

"Together? But we are together," Grace responds, confusion evident in her voice.

"No, it's not what I mean." I feel a wet drop go down my chest.

"What do you mean?" Grace inquires, her tone tinged with uncertainty.

My heart is racing. "I want to live with you."

Grace holds eye contact with me for what seems like an eternity. She embraces me tightly, and I feel the warmth of her body enveloping me. With her glossy eyes reflecting and water droplets increasing on my body, she sits straight and looks at me.

"Yes! Finally! Although, I don't think my dog would appreciate your cat's presence."

"I'm thrilled about this."

"Oh my god, I'm so glad you asked," she exclaims, embracing me, and kissing my left cheek.

"Wake up, Nairb!" Jim says, waving his hand in front of my face.

"Sorry, my mind wandered. Can you repeat that?" I sniff, then gaze at Jim, my eyes glossy.

"Hey, did I catch you crying?"

"Don't be silly. My eyes are watering because of something."

"It's okay if you did."

"I'm okay," I say, looking past Jim's right shoulder.

"Nairb?"

I notice that Jim is looking at the clock on the brown wood-paneled wall behind me. "Do you think we can visit my house and see Dawna?" Jim asks.

"I think it's not wise to do it now."

"Despite it not being a good idea, I need to experience it for myself. And if something doesn't seem right, we can always return."

"Well, alright, but I wouldn't go right now."

The earth trembled, causing the lights to flicker and the fireplace fire to die out, plunging us into darkness.

We sat in silence, listening to the wind howling through the cracks in the door until the shaking stopped.

Jim's eyes are wet with emotion, and a teardrop slips down his cheek.

We hear a loud noise.

"What was that?" Jim asks, his voice hushed.

"It could be a snowstorm, but I'm not sure," I reply.

"Okay, let's go to my place." Jim says.

The sound of humming fills the room as the light moves like a reflection on water and we step in.

"Turn around!" Jim shouts, and I do.

The sound of my footsteps on the living room's hardwood floor made a distinct thump.

"She's still at work." Jim gestures for me to have a seat on the couch.

The sound of a key being inserted into the keyhole makes me pause just before I can sit down on the black leather couch. Our heads turn simultaneously, and I notice Jim turning red in my peripheral vision as we observe the lock moving.

The door creaks open, and Dawna steps inside, grasping the smooth, solid wooden door and swinging it closed behind her. With a heavy sigh, she throws her purse down on the brown bench and leans against the door, her back to us.

She looks up and calls out, "Jim. Nairb."

A dark line of thick smoke pours from Dawna's mouth as she makes a loud scree sound, splattering against the ceiling with the sound of cracking. A dark shadow gradually emerges above her head, growing more defined with each passing moment. The bloody eyes of the dark shadow lock onto me as Dawna drops to the ground.

Jim and I share a quick look, and we both feel the dampness on our faces.

"Nairb, I've been waiting for you," the shadow says in a low voice, eyes glowing.

The shadow launches at me as a bright figure appears in front of me, acting as a wall. The shadow splatters against it. The shadow tries to grab me around its sides, but the shadow's dark, sharp, pointy hands wrap around it, keeping the shadow from going forward.

Jim, hurry, and grab Dawna! The crack will close soon!"

He picks Dawna up as the wind blows, causing the curtains to flutter and Jim to slow down.

I gesture for him to go through the crack, and he nods.

As Jim walks into the crack, the windows shatter, and a loud growl emanates from the shadow.

"Nairb!" Jim shouts.

Stepping back, I turn around to see Jim's hands grasping his black hair in horror, his eyes wide.

I see the crack closing.

CHAPTER 8: DAWNA

As I extend my arms, I watch as the shadow draws closer and closer, until it is right in front of me. I roll and land on cottage floor, the rough wood scratching against my skin, before coming to a stop on my back with my hands splayed out. As I raise my head, the crack in front of me seals shut, and the only sound left is my breathing.

Jim runs toward me. "Are you okay?"

"Yes, I'm okay," I say, standing up, catching my breath.

"That was close. What was that thing?"

"I don't know. Where is Dawna?"

"I put her down on the couch. She is still unconscious," Jim says.

"This stuff is baffling," I announce.

I take a quick look at Dawna, confirming that she is unconscious, then walk over to the fridge by the far wall in the kitchen and grab two cans of beer.

"Here, catch," I say, gently underhand tossing one to Jim.

Catching it, Jim expresses his gratitude with a quick, "Thanks."

I flick open my can and hear the satisfying hiss of the carbonation. I take a sip and start walking toward Jim.

"Since I got these powers, things have been getting serious around me. I have so many questions, but I have no one to ask." I walk past Jim and sit down on a brown couch by the fireplace.

As Jim approaches, he cracks open his beer, the sound of carbonation releasing, filling the space between us.

Sitting down beside me on my right, he takes a sip and says, "Don't worry, Nairb. Eventually, you'll get your answers." He takes another long gulp and sinks back into the couch cushions.

"I really want to believe you're right," I say with a sigh, looking over at Dawna, who is beginning to stir.

I turn my head back to Jim.

"What are you guys doing? What happened?" Dawna asks, slowly trying to sit up.

"What do you mean, what happened? You don't remember?" Jim asks, gazing at her seriously.

"No, the last thing I remember is stepping outside to talk to those officers."

Dawna moves her head around. "Wait! Where am I?"

"You are safe in a secluded cottage," Jim answers.

"What about Connie?"

"She's okay, from what we know." I glance at Jim.

"It was really strange, you guys. I don't remember anything; I just felt like I was being held."

Jim and I exchange a quick, meaningful glance, then return our eyes to Dawna.

Standing up, I say, "I'm glad you're back."

Jim walks over to Dawna and settles beside her, softly kissing her cheek.

"What are we going to do, Nairb?" Jim asks, his thumb absentmindedly stroking Dawna's leg. The intensity of Jim's gaze is palpable as I pace, his eyes tracking my every movement.

"Do you have any idea when we'll be able to catch up with Patty?"

"We can go there now."

"Wait! Who's Patty?"

"Jim's friend; maybe she can help."

Jim turns to Dawna. "I will tell you later."

"Jim, I don't know where to go," I say.

"Do you remember our playhouse?"

"Yes, I do."

"Go there."

"What do you mean, go there?" Dawna asks.

"I will fill you in later," Jim replies.

The playhouse lingers in my thoughts, the creaking of the old, weathered wood resonating. With a sudden noise, Dawna's head whips around, and the flickering light reveals her startled expression.

"Whoa, what is that?"

Jim walks up to Dawna and nods toward the crack, saying, "Just follow me," before disappearing inside. Dawna locks eyes with me for a moment, and then she is gone. Walking toward them, I pause to take in the surrounding sights. Looking through the tunnel of light, I see Dawna and Jim standing on the yellow sand of the playground, staring in my direction. The sight brings back a flood of memories of Grace.

#

"Are you sure this slide is safe for me to go down, Nairb?" Grace asks nervously.

"I have no doubt," I reply, my tone showing my complete certainty.

Her hand slips from mine, and the sound of her laughter fills the air as she runs onto the sandy ground. She climbs up the ladder inside the playhouse to reach the top. Without hesitation, she darts toward the yellow, curvy plastic slide and goes down, hands in the air, a grin on her face, and the rush of wind in her hair.

Grace halts on the sand, then darts off the slide, her feet kicking up sand as she sprints over to me.

She stops abruptly in front of me, wheezing, and confesses, "I always wanted to do that."

"Go down a slide?"

"No, silly, until now, I was always too scared to raise my hands up."

Walking alongside me, Grace reaches for my right hand, intertwines our fingers, and we continue along our path.

Letting out an enormous sigh, I step through the crack and onto the sandy ground. The playhouse is only a few feet ahead.

"Why did it take you so long?" Jim asks.

"I was thinking about something."

"Nairb, how long have you been able to do this?" Dawna exclaims, rushing over to me.

As I turn to her, I see my reflection in her wide eyes. "Not long," I say.

"You can go anywhere?" she asks incredulously, impressed by the possibilities.

"Only to locations I can picture." I turn to Jim. "How far is it to Patty's?"

"It's close to here, just up that street," Jim says, pointing in its direction.

Jim approaches Dawna, and I follow them, leaving the sand behind and stepping onto the asphalt path that curves toward the street. The moon above casts a glow on our path, and I can't help but notice the brilliance of the stars in the sky. As I look up at them, one twinkles, and a tear rolls down my cheek. I crinkle my nose and take a shallow breath.

"Nairb, are you okay?" Jim asks, his expression worried.

I nod.

As we stroll together, I feel Jim's piercing gaze fixed on me.

"I'm just cold," I reply, rubbing my hands together and avoiding eye contact. "When did you first meet Patty?"

"She made my first fake ID card."

"Really?"

"Yes, really."

"I just don't see you as a rebel."

"You're not the only one with a rebel past."

"Are we nearly there yet?" I say, as we step onto a street.

"Yes, it is the black house on your left."

"Black?"

"Yes, no comment."

"You never told me about her, Jim?" Dawna says.

"There was no need to say anything; plus, I forgot."

"Uh-hum." Dawna's skin color turns red, and she turns away from him.

"I see a black house. Is that it?" I inquire.

"Yes."

The sound of thunder echoes down the street, and the lamps on the post sputter out, casting the area into darkness.

"Jim, come on! We need to move faster," I say, my heart racing. As the lamps flicker off, the stars emerge one by one, casting a dim glow.

Our footsteps reverberate loudly as our pace quickens, heading toward the black house with its bright lights in the driveway. The sudden darkness is accompanied by a cacophony of shattering glass and exploding bulbs.

I take a quick look over my shoulder and see the shadow's red eyes glinting in the darkness.

The wind is so strong that Jim's words are almost lost, but he yells, "We're almost there."

As we step onto the driveway, a chill runs down my spine as I feel the looming presence behind us.

The darkness is so thick that we can feel it pressing against our skin like a physical force. My palms are slick with sweat, and my heart thuds against my ribcage as I lock eyes with the shadow, and I breathe heavily. Unexpectedly, it stops in its tracks.

"I wonder what caused it to stop?" I say.

"It doesn't matter why, but it did." Jim says, out of breath. "Let's go."

He leads the way to a black wooden door, the sound of his footsteps echoing on the driveway.

"I didn't expect your friend to be so solemn," I state.

"She was not before; this is new." Jim says, knocking.

A woman opens the door and greets Jim with a smile, her gaze then sweeping over us. Around six feet with black hair and slim.

"Meet Patty," Jim says to us. "Patty, this is my wife Dawna and our friend Nairb."

"Nice to meet you. By the way, there's someone with red eyes trying to hammer their way in through my force field," she says, pointing at the driveway.

We whip our heads around in perfect unison, alerted by the growling sound of the shadow trying to take flight. We discover that the property is inside a massive bubble when it hit the driveway's force shield. The noise gets louder with each bounce from the shield. I stand frozen in fear as the shadow's gaze locks on me, my heart racing, and my ears ringing with its pounding.

PATTY

"Don't just stand there," Patty beckons, holding the door open.

In unity, our heads swivel toward her. Jim and Dawna lead the way inside, and I follow closely behind. Patty closes the door behind her, the sound of the latch clicking shut echoing in the small room.

"I don't even recognize this place anymore," Jim observes, noticing all the changes.

"I've added things to keep the evil spirits away, although I was skeptical at first. But once I saw things, my beliefs changed. I'll tell you about it another time. What brings you here?" she asks, guiding us to the living room.

"I tried to explain on the phone, but now things have become more complicated with the recent incident you just witnessed."

"I also saw you guys on TV, so I have an idea of what you need. But for the spirit chasing you, you'll need more help. Fortunately, I know someone who can assist you. He helped me, so I'm sure he can help you too, but first, let's change how you look."

"What do you mean, how we look?" Jim's gaze flickers past us and lands on Patty.

"You don't want to match the police description. Have a seat on the couch, and I'll fetch something." Patty gestures to the furniture.

Jim looks at us and strolls toward the inviting black leather couch, beckoning us to follow suit. We all sit down, with Dawna in the middle. As I lean back on the couch, the sound of my fingers tapping against the cushion fills the room. The black brick wall looms in front of me as Jim and Dawna lean back, and I can't help but feel a sense of dread.

Dawna's leg brushes lightly against mine, and I turn to look at her.

I whisper, barely audible, "What?"

"Look." Dawna moves her eyes down.

As I gaze toward the floor, a white cat catches my eye, and I find myself fixated on its every movement. I watch Dawna momentarily before glancing back at the cat, which is now almost at my right leg. It's white, soft fur brushes against my leg, and I reach out to pet it. I feel the long wisps beneath my fingertips as I stroke it a few times before leaning back.

"Betse seems to like you," Patty says, reentering the room, carrying a pile of items. "So, who's up for a new look? I've got everything we need right here," she exclaims, putting everything down in a heap on a chair.

Jim and I look at each other, our heads swiveling in harmony. A moment of silence passes before Jim breaks it.

"I'm ready. What's the plan?" he asks confidently.

"Let me put these drops in your eyes first," Patty says as she approaches him a small bottle in her hand.

"Drops?"

"Green is the only color I have right now. Jim, lean back and close your eyes until I say to open them, or you'll risk going blind."

Dawna and I watch silently as Patty carefully administers the drops into Jim's eyes.

"Don't open until I say so," Patty reminds him as she steps away from the couch.

With a smile, Patty asks, "Who's next?"

"I will be," I announce.

Turning my head, I catch a glimpse of relief flickering across Dawna's face.

I look at Patty. "Put your head back, Nairb."

Patty leans over, holding the bottle a few inches away

from my face, and I tilt my head back. I wince as she squeezes the bottle, and a few droplets of the green fluid hit my eyes. The warmth spreads as the fluid splashes against my eyeballs. Closing my lids, I am enveloped in a comforting warmth, and I can sense a subtle flickering of light and dark behind them. The swift movements cause an occasional sensation of something prickly in my eyes, as if small particles are flying around me.

"Dawna, you're next." Patty administers the drops to Dawna, then instructs her to keep her eyes closed until she tells her she can open them.

"I'll be right back," she says, and the sound of her footsteps diminish until there is only silence. A series of clinks and clanks are followed by the sound of a drawer being opened as she searches for something.

As the silence descends once again, I strain to hear any remote noise. A minute later, the sound of footsteps grows louder.

"You guys can open your eyes now."

I open mine slowly, and Patty's features gradually come into view. I turn my head toward Jim, and a few seconds later, he angles his glance toward me.

"Your eyes are green, Jim."

"Yours too."

We both look at Dawna. "What? Is there anything on my face?" she asked, reaching up to touch her cheek. Touching her face and turning her head multiple times.

"No, Dawna, your eyes are green," Jim said.

"Really?"

"Yes."

Patty hands Dawna a small pocket mirror. With the mirror in hand, Dawna gazes at her reflection and gently presses her fingers against her right cheek.

"Jim, you're so right," she said, widening her eyes to show appreciation.

Patty walks over to us, one by one, and places a small, round, pink, shiny tablet in our right hands.

"What's this?" I inquire.

"This will change your face."

"My face?"

"Swallow the pill, and then relax on the couch. I'll be back soon," Patty says, walking away.

The three of us look at one another and then down at the pill in our hand. Jim tosses the pill in his mouth, and he swallows. Dawna as I do the same, and then we all lean back on the couch.

A few minutes later, there is a sensation like someone is pinching me in different places on my face, followed by the agonizing sensation of being cut. I hear Dawna scream.

"Just be strong, Dawna," I say loudly, gripping the leather cushions with my hand.

My feet push me further into the couch. Feeling the constant facial movements, I look at the ceiling to try and distract myself. I hear my nails snap, and then everything suddenly stops, as if a brake has been pulled.

"Are you guys okay?"

"Yes," they both answer at the same time.

I lift my head, then try to pull my body up. I turn and see Jim and Dawna trying to do the same, but they don't look like themselves anymore.

"Jim, your face looks different."

"You too, Nairb. Dawna, you too," Jim says, lifting his hand and touching his face.

Dawna lifts her hands and starts touching her face.

"Nairb, I see red lights at the window."

I turn my head to look, just as there is a knock at the black door. A rapid thumping starts in my chest, and a streak of sweat erupts.

CHAPTER 9: SHOPPING

Patty rushes toward the door, shouting, "I'm coming!" As she opens the door, I catch a glimpse of a person wearing a black hat with a shiny, silver star-shaped pin on their chest.

"Officer, how may I assist you today?" Patty asks.

"We received a report stating that people who fit the description of some criminals we are looking for have been seen in this vicinity."

"As you can see, only my friends are here, sitting on the couch."

He quickly glances at us before retracting his head, saying, "Apologies for the disturbance. Have a pleasant evening," then tipping his hat and striding off.

Patty closes the door and walks toward us.

"That was insane!" I exclaim, still buzzing with excitement. "He did not know who we are!"

"You look completely different. I was not worried."

"Yes, but still."

Dawna grabs the pocket mirror beside her and lifts it to her face.

"Wow, my face has changed. I have no wrinkles!" she says, touching her cheeks.

Jim turns his head and agrees, "You're absolutely right, and you're so beautiful."

"I wasn't before?" Dawna's voice rises with disbelief.

"You always were, I'm just saying . . ."

She taps her fingers on the couch. "Saying what, exactly?"

Patty and I exchange a quick glance and then look away.

"I'm just saying," Jim says, blushing, "You look as beautiful as ever!"

"Uh-hum."

"Excuse me for interrupting, but I'd like to take a picture," Patty exclaims, revealing a black camera from behind her back.

"Picture?"

"Yes, you will need new identification to travel safely. Now, don't move."

Patty takes a picture of each of us.

"Here is the address. Vlad is expecting you. Come back in a few hours to pick up your new IDs." Patty walks over to Jim and hands him a piece of paper.

"Thanks," Jim says, taking it and standing up.

As Jim looks over the paper, he steals a few glances in my direction. As I get on my feet, I hear Dawna shuffling behind me.

"When can we see him?" Jim asks.

"Anytime, it's a blue house," Patty replies.

"Don't panic about what you see at his house."

"Don't worry."

Memories of my shopping trip flood my mind, causing a crack to appear, and I see the light glinting in Patty's eyes.

Jim looks at the crack, surprise on his face at seeing the grocery store. "This is not the cottage?"

"No, it's not. We have to get some food."

Jim briefly glances at me before disappearing into the crack, leaving me to see him standing between aisles on a white tile floor. Following a brief pause, Dawna follows a few seconds later.

"Nice meeting you," I say to Patty as I turned to look at her. Then, I shift my gaze to the crack and walked toward it, stepping inside.

Standing next to Jim, I turn around and see Patty waving her hand. We wave goodbye, and her image gradually shrinks and disappears.

The silence is so complete that we can hear our own breathing, and we exchange a look.

"Can you get the shopping cart, Dawna?" I ask, showing her the direction she needs to go. Then I turn back to Jim.

Hearing the cracking coming from Jim's mouth, I exclaim, "Jim, what are you doing? Put those chips down."

"Sorry," he says, his mouth full.

"Come, follow me."

As I walk down the aisle, the sound of my footsteps echo around me. I see Dawna pushing the shopping cart toward us.

I reach for the bread loaf on the second shelf, feeling the softness in my hands, and place it gently in the cart, just as Dawna pulls up beside me.

"What are we getting?" she asks, with a hint of impatience in her voice.

"For now, only the essentials," I reply, placing a six-pack of beer bottles in the cart.

Dawna's silent gaze meets mine and she grins, "I don't think beer is essential," then she turns away and takes a box of crackers from a shelf and puts them in the cart.

Carrying a stack of juice cartons, Jim makes his way over and placed them in the cart. As we stroll through the store, we gather an assortment of items and loaded them into the cart until it can no longer hold any more.

"Nairb," Jim says, peeling a banana and taking a bite, "Do you think we're good?"

"Yes."

"I'm just going to grab one more thing," he says, his footsteps fading as he walks away.

My gaze shifts to the front of the cart, and at that moment, a crack materializes, casting a beam of light onto the produce section. Through the crack, I glimpse the image of a couch in a cottage and observe the snowflakes gracefully cascading behind a window.

"Ladies first," I say, giving Dawna a polite nod.

Dawna strolls through, looking at me as I push the cart toward her.

"Hey, Nairb, I just heard a noise, and something is moving." I look back and spot a shadow.

As the shadow soars toward Jim, the sound of glass shattering echoes through the air.

"Jim, run," I shout, and he immediately drops the banana he was holding, his fingers fumbling in his haste.

Gripping her hair, Dawna screams, "Jim, hurry!" Her voice is filled with fear and urgency.

The sound of a growl fills the air, getting louder and closer as it threatens to overtake Jim, who is being chased by the shadow with the intense red eyes. With a sudden burst of motion, the shadow extends its sharp fingers and releases an object, hurtling it toward Jim. The impact on his back pushes him forward, his body instinctively finding solace in the embrace of the closing crack.

"Jim!" Dawna screams, piercing the silence.

I catch him, wrapping my arms tightly around him, feeling his heartbeat against my chest.

"Please place him on the couch carefully," Dawna instructs, her voice gentle yet firm.

I gently move his body, feeling its weightlessness, while his feet softly scrape the wooden floor, creating a gentle squeak. As I lay him down on the couch, my eyes catch sight of a menacing black object protruding from his back. I yank it off and forcefully hurl it against the wall, watching it collide with a resounding thud. I carefully lay him on his back, glancing at Dawna quickly before returning my attention to Jim.

"Don't worry, buddy," I tell him, my hand firmly gripping his arm.

"There's an issue," I say, holding Jim's arm and glancing at Dawna.

"What is it?"

"I don't feel a draining."

"Can you please clarify?" she says, her eyes watery.

"It's not draining me like before," seeing Jim turning pale.

"Jim, where is the address?

"My left pocket," he mutters so quietly that it is almost inaudible.

I reach out and take the crumpled paper from his pocket, feeling its smooth texture on my fingertips, before standing up.

I look at Dawna, my eyes conveying my promise. "I'll be back."

"Wait!" she pleads; her eyes wide with fear. "Where are you headed?" she asks curiously.

"I think it is a good idea to pay this Vlad a visit," I explain, looking down at the paper and then at Dawna. "Luckily, I'm quite familiar with this place." With a nonchalant gesture, I casually flick the paper with my finger. "Stay with him," I firmly instruct, my finger pointing directly at Jim as a silent command.

As the address area crosses my mind, a crack manifests before me. Stepping onto the cracked gray sidewalk on the other side, my shoes immediately register the rough, bumpy surface. The sensation of cool droplets on my arm makes me glance upwards, where I see the dark clouds looming overhead.

My eyes light up as I exclaim, "Great! If my memory serves me right, the street should be after that bend up ahead."

As I start walking, I feel drops of water hitting the top of my head with increasing force, splashing faster. As my pace quickens, I hear the increasing patter of rain hitting the ground. The sight of the street ahead fills me with excitement, and I break into a sprint, my breath creating a cloud.

A blue sign with a number is affixed to a one-story gray house. I head toward the front door, the soft, yellow light emanating from the bulb above it reflecting off the pavement. As I knock, I hear the intensifying splashing of droplets against the ground. With a slight groan, the door swings open to the right. An old man materializes before me, his chest-length beard a tangle of white curls.

"Hi, I'm looking for Vlad."

"I'm Vlad."

"Patty has sent me here. I'm Nairb. She said you might be able to help me."

"Yes, I was expecting you. Please come in. Can I get you a cup of tea?"

"No, thank you," I say urgently, my voice filled with panic. "I can't heal my friend for some reason. He's been hit by a shadow figure that has been following us."

"Take a seat," he says, escorting me to the living room.

I sit on the plush, white, leather-looking couch, and Vlad plops down beside me.

"Now, tell me what happened to your friend?"

As I recount the events that occurred just moments ago, Vlad's full attention is fixed on me.

Getting up from the couch, Vlad saunters over to an ancient, black cabinet, its surface marred with deep scratch marks. With anticipation, he opens it and retrieves a bottle holding a dark, mysterious liquid. As I continued telling my story, my eyes track his movements. Vlad closes the cabinet, the creak of the hinges filling the room, and settles back into the plush couch, his body sinking into its comfortable embrace.

As he speaks, with a serious expression on his face, he passes me a hazy bottle.

"Make sure your friend drinks this. It's a quick remedy for his condition. You can take care of him with your healing later."

I feel the cool glass of the bottle in my hand. Vlad leans back on the couch and locks eyes with me.

"Tell me the rest."

Leaning back, I cross my arms and dive into the narrative of what has transpired. His nodding is gentle and frequent, showing his familiarity with my words. With his arms on his knees, he leans forward, his body language conveying his intensity.

"Nairb, you have been given mysterious gifts. Their purpose is known only to your guardian."

"My guardian?"

"Yes, your guardian. Were you very close to someone, and they left you?"

"Yes," I reply, with glossy eyes, "My wife Grace and I were in a car accident."

"The bond is strong, and she is with you even now."

"Really?" I exclaim, my eyebrows shooting up in surprise. "Grace, it's Nairb," standing up, calling her.

"Sit back down; it's not that simple."

"Vlad, what do you mean?" I ask, my voice filled with confusion.

"Visit where she rests. Call for her alone, and she will appear."

"Really?" I say, my voice tinged with a mix of surprise and excitement.

He hands me the amulet, leans slightly, and instructs me to wear it for protection as my guardian guides me further.

"Really! Thank you so much."

"You are welcome. Give Patty my best."

"I will," I declare, rising from my seat and recalling the image of Jim in the cottage.

A crack appears, filling the room with a blinding light, revealing a vision of Dawna sitting beside Jim, who is still laying down.

As a loud bang reverberates, our attention is drawn to the dark window, where two fiery red eyes glare back at us.

"Don't worry about it," Vlad reassures me, his gaze fixed on mine.

"Oh, okay," I reply, feeling a sense of relief. "Thank you for your help."

Turning my head, I catch sight of the crack, and as I step into it, I feel the smoothness of the polished wooden floor beneath my feet. I turn around and wave my hand, signaling goodbye. "Bye, thank you again."

Vlad waves his hand, a flicker of movement catching the corner of his eye, and calmly walks away.

CHAPTER 10: HEAL

Dawna's eyes meet mine. "You're back."

"Yes," I say, my voice filled with anticipation. "How is he doing?"

"He finally went to sleep, but his body is drenched in a constant layer of sweat."

I walk over to Jim and pour a few drops of the liquid from the bottle into his mouth.

"Jim will be fine in a few hours," I assure her, my voice filled with confidence. "I'll be able to heal him then. Go get some rest. There is a comfortable bed in the adjacent room," I tell her, pointing in that direction.

"Okay," Dawna said, getting up, placing a towel down beside Jim. Inquisitively, she points to the amulet hanging from my neck and asks me what it is.

"I'll explain later."

She walks away, the sound of her footsteps fading into the distance.

I reach out and gently pat Jim's leg, attempting to reassure him. "You will be okay, buddy," I whisper.

Jim's eyes flutter open for a moment, a flicker of recognition in his gaze before he turns his head and closes his eyes.

I walk over to the white leather couch, the softness of the cushions inviting me to lie down and rest. When I eventually open my eyes, squinting against the bright light, I raise my hand to shield my face, and sit up. I look at Jim, his peaceful face illuminated by the morning light, still lost in slumber. I walk over to him and gently grasp his weightless arm. Instantly, I feel a sharp, stinging sensation, as if a mosquito is biting me, draining the energy from my hands.

The moment the draining stops, my vision blurs, making me feel lightheaded. As I gaze up at Jim, I am relieved to see that the pallor has faded from his face. I give his leg a reassuring pat before getting up and making my way back to the inviting couch, where I once again sink into its plush cushions. As I lay down, darkness envelops my vision, leaving me with a void of sight. A soft voice catches my attention, followed by a forceful nudge on my shoulder and a louder voice.

I open my eyes and see Jim standing near me. "Jim, you're up."

"Dawna!" I exclaim, sitting up, my voice filled with surprise and delight. "Jim is awake!" I shout. "How are you feeling?"

"I'm feeling good," Jim says, giving me a reassuring pat on the back.

Dawna's rapid footsteps echo through the room, reverberating against the wooden floor.

"Jim!" she calls out, her voice filled with a mixture of excitement and urgency. With a burst of energy, she dashes toward her husband, ready to embrace him.

They hug each other, and Dawna kisses him all over his face, leaving red lipstick in her wake.

Dawna locks eyes with him and inquires, "How are you feeling?"

"I'm good."

"I'm glad to hear it. We were worried about you," she says.

Jim gives a confused look.

"Why?" he asks, his voice filled with concern. "What happened?"

"You don't remember?" Dawna exclaims, her eyes widening in surprise.

"No, the last thing I remember is the feeling of adrenaline coursing through my veins as I sprinted toward the crack, desperate to escape the pursuing shadow. Did something else happen?"

Dawna and I exchange a quick, relieved glance, affirming our sentiments.

"I'll fix us some breakfast," Dawna announces, then heads to the kitchen.

I tell Jim about his experiences and the events that transpired. His undivided attention is palpable, as he listens intently, never interrupting. I go over to the sharp, black triangular object that was lunged in his back, which I pulled out and threw against the wall, to bring it over and show him.

Touching it, a shiver runs down my back, sending shivers down my spine as a cacophony of hushed voices fill the air, accompanied by an intense, piercing cold.

In a rush, I jump to my feet and carelessly set the object on the round, small black table beside the wall.

Jim's piercing gaze meets mine as he asks what happened.

"I can't describe it accurately, but I sensed a powerful and distressing vision of pain."

With a gentle whir, the object starts to levitate, defying all expectations.

"Look!" Jim points excitedly at the mysterious object, hovering above the table.

We both turn our heads, lock our eyes for a moment, and then turn back.

I move my hand closer to it. "One end feels smooth, but the other is pointy, and I see that it is has a bit of red liquid on it. I think that sharp side was edged in you."

As I adjust my stance, the object tumbles back onto the table. Its impact echoes a chilling resemblance to a spoon being dropped, evoking a whisper of impending doom.

"Did you hear that?" I exclaim, my heart racing with the unknown.

"Yes, I heard it," Jim confirms.

"What was that?"

"I don't know, but we should move away, just in case."

"Good idea."

Stepping back, we both continue to gaze at the object, captivated by its presence for a few minutes.

"I don't think it'll do anything else."

I give Jim a nod. "Yeah, you're probably right."

"Breakfast is ready," Dawna shouts, her voice echoing through the cabin.

"Come on, let's go," I say, reassuring Jim with a pat on the shoulder as I stride toward Dawna.

Jim walks behind me, his footsteps drumming against the brown hardwood floor. At the light-yellow wooden round table, we pull out the dark-yellow wooden chairs and get comfortable. Jim sits a few feet beside me, and Dawna sits across from me. As I look down, I smell the delicious aroma of cheese and tomato wafting up from two perfectly assembled sandwiches.

"Looks good, Dawna," I say, grabbing the sandwich.

"Thanks, dinner will be better. The ham is defrosting on the counter."

"This is good, honey. Thank you," Jim says.

"I think we should go to Patty's after we finish," my gaze shifts between them.

"Why do you want to go to Patty's?" Dawna widens her eyes.

"To grab our IDs, plus I want to say hello to my parents, and I miss my mom's baked muffins."

"Okay, sounds like a plan," Dawna replies, then resumes biting into her sandwich.

"I'll wash up. Do you have an extra shirt here?" Jim asks.

"Yes, I do. There is one in the bedroom."

"Great, thanks."

We carry on eating for a couple more minutes, when I hear a scraping noise from a chair as Jim stands up.

"I'm going to wash up," he says, heading to the bathroom.

I take a few more bites before deciding to get up. As I walk, I catch a glimpse of something dark moving past the window, causing me to halt and fixate my gaze on the kitchen window.

"What's wrong?" Dawna asks.

I put a finger over my mouth, indicating for her to stay quiet.

Dawna turns her head toward the window, and we both gaze out for a minute. "What?" she whispers, "I just see falling snow, creating a winter wonderland."

I shrug at her and muttered, "Sorry, nothing," before making my way to the sink and carefully placing my dish inside.

A thunderous roar echoes through the air, causing the glass window to vibrate.

The singing noise catches our ears, and we look in the direction of the thick, white substance leaking from under the washroom door. As the roar resounds once more, Dawna springs to her feet, accompanied by the unmistakable sound of wood scraping against the floor.

"Nairb, your amulet is glowing a bright blue," Dawna informs me.

"Stand behind me," I instruct, and without hesitation, Dawna does as I say. I see her hand grasp the pink broom that was leaning against the wall.

With my eyes scanning the room, my head sways from left to right, while my left hand gently holds on to Dawna behind me. I take small, cautious steps backward.

The washroom door flies open, reverberating with a sharp knock as the handle makes contact with the wall behind it. Our heads snap toward the loud banging sound coming from inside, and we see a thick, white cloud of steam billowing out, gradually dissipating. Bursting with energy, Jim slides out on his knees, arms outstretched, his booming voice filling the space as he announces he is ready.

Dawna moves her hand inward, her voice filled with urgency. "Quick, come here."

"What's with the pale faces and serious expressions? And Dawna, why are you holding a broom up?" Jim asks.

We hear a piercing, high pitch scrape near the kitchen window, our heads instinctively turning toward the sound.

"Oh, that's why," Jim says, getting up off his knees. I feel the rush of wind as he runs past me to my right side. Jim looks at Dawna skeptically, his eyebrows furrowing.

"I don't think the broom will do anything," he says.

Dawna looks at the broom, its worn bristles and splintered handle. "You're right, dear," she agrees, dropping it with a clatter.

The sound of shattering glass fills the air as a wall of black smoke emerges, obstructing the view like a solid barrier. The smoke enters the room with such force that it feels as if it is being sucked in, colliding with the ceiling above us. As I look in that direction, I am met with a chilling sight: blood-red eyes fixed upon me. As my hair sways to the left, I watch the kitchen table glide across the smooth wooden floor, tearing apart my newspaper, scattering its pages throughout the room. There is a light tap on my right shoulder, causing me to turn towards Jim.

"Quick, the crack," Jim shouts.

The crack appears, slicing through the thick black smoke.

"Dawna, go quickly. Jim, you go after her."

"What about you?"

As I push Jim forward, I yell, "I'll be right behind you!"

With my hand shielding my head, I make my way toward the crack, stooping slightly as I push my way through. As I turn around, a dense and ominous cloud of smoke slithers through the window, like a sinister serpent. Inside, the room is filled with an eerie presence, emphasized by the haunting, blood-red eyes that stare at me, making me take a step back and feel the slow, rhythmic pounding in my chest. It charges toward me with alarming speed, as if I were its intended target, but then it was abruptly halted by an invisible force field, resulting in a jarring metallic collision.

The dark cloud is just a few meters away, moving side to side, with the bloody eyes fixed on me until the crack starts to close. When it does, I turn and face Dawna and Jim.

"Where are we?" Jim asks, looking around.

"Playland."

"Playland?" Jim mutters.

"Yes, Playland. I came here as a kid with my parents."

"Interesting. Can we go to Patty's?" Jim inquires.

"Yes," I reply. "But we have a problem."

"What problem?" Jim gazes at me.

"The crack is not working."

"What do you mean it's not working?"

"Nothing is happening, Jim; I'm trying, but nothing is happening."

"Great," Jim turns around. "You couldn't pick a better place?"

"It's not like I had time to think about it. This just popped into my head."

"How far are we from home?" Jim asks, looking at the rollercoaster.

"About three hours. It has been a while, Jim."

"Okay, let's start walking. In which direction, Nairb?" Jim looks in every direction.

"Go left."

"Jim, can we go on a ride first?"

"No, Dawna, not right now," Jim replies.

Jim sees Dawna drop her head in disappointment.

"Fine, let's go for one ride."

Dawna looks up. "Really?"

"Yes, really. Only one, though. Are you okay with this, Nairb?"

I nod my head in agreement.

"Yay! Thanks, guys!" Dawna exclaims. "Fun is in store for you."

"Off to the roller coaster we go!" Jim declares.

As we walk for a few minutes, the colorful lights and excited voices coming from the booth for the ride become more prominent.

"Luckily, I have a few coins jingling in my pocket," Jim announces.

"Look," I whisper, pointing to a police officer up ahead.

All eyes turn to him.

"You know this is weird that no one knows who we are," I whisper to Jim, as the bustling sounds of people going about their own activities surround us.

"Yes, I know. It feels strange," Jim responds, his hand brushing against the cold metal railing as we start moving a few steps in line.

As Dawna looks around, a sense of paranoia settles in, as if an unseen threat is chasing her.

Approaching the booth, Jim eagerly purchases three tickets, and we pass through the green metallic gate.

We patiently wait, observing as a passerby briefly locks eyes with us. Eventually, the ride arrives and comes to a stop right in front of us, where the previous occupants disembark.

As I near the roller coaster, I am surprised at how tiny it is compared to others I've seen. Only four people can ride in the two connected blue carts. Walking toward a cart, Jim and Dawna position themselves in the front, leaving me to sit alone in the back. The cushions, resembling black sponges, emerge from the bottom of the floor, immediately pressing me into the back wall of the seat. I am held down, like I am anchored to the ground.

With a sudden jerk, the ride lurches forward, then smoothly gains momentum. I place my hands on the top of the cart.

As we ascend the rails, the rhythmic clicking of the metal beneath our feet grows louder, and I tilt my head to take in the breathtaking scenery below.

Turning my head in the opposite direction, I ask Jim if he notices the black shape in the sky to the right.

"It's most likely just a rain cloud," he responds, then faces forward again.

A few seconds later, I say, "Jim, it's moving toward us."

Jim looks up. "You are right, Nairb, it is moving."

Our eyes widen as we gaze at it, realizing it is gradually moving in our direction.

A sinking feeling washes over me as I clench my hands against the cart's front wall.

Jim and Dawna hold on tightly to their cart as well. "Crap!"

Seconds later, the ride begins hurtling down the track, picking up speed with each passing second, accompanied by the rapid clicks and vibrations of the cart.

Dawna's hair is whipping around in all directions as she shouts, "Don't be afraid, you guys!" Raising her hands up, she yells, "Yay!"

Finally, we reach a flat part on the track, and Jim is looking all around in the sky.

"Where is it?" he shouts.

"What are you looking for?" Dawna inquires.

"A dark cloud," he replies.

"You mean the one headed this way?" Dawna says, pointing to it.

"Yes. Nairb," he says, his voice filled with panic, "There is nothing we can do."

As it comes closer, I can see its bloody eyes gazing at me, and the cart is being pulled up with a loud clicking sound.

"Can you fire it or something?"

"I'm sorry, but I can't. I lost that ability," I tell them, as we go higher.

"Great, just great."

"I'm sure we will find a way out of this," Dawna says calmly, trying to ease our worries. "Is there an escape route?"

"We are on a roller coaster!" Jim exclaims.

"Jim, there's no need to panic. Dawna is right. Quickly, brace yourself!" I shout.

With our hands resting on the front of our carts, we feel the vibrations, and Dawna's hair flies around. As silence surrounds us, the fast clicking and rolling wheels grow louder, filling the void. After a minute, I feel the smooth glide as we roll back onto the flat track.

"Jim, once we finish, just run straight ahead; I see a train close to here."

"Do you think we can make it?"

"Do you have a better idea?"

Jim's expression conveys a silent no. He briefly glances at me, then shifts his gaze elsewhere and remains silent.

"Nairb, it's approaching!" he exclaims, pointing up at the shadow, his eyes widening in alarm.

Dawna's gaze fixates on it, then turns to me, her eyes filled with anticipation, as if waiting for my guidance.

The shadow slowly advances toward us, causing Dawna to scream in terror. I attempt to strike it as it circles above us, emitting a low growl. The punch's impact sends a surge of coldness through my hand, reminiscent of gripping an ice cube. Amid the ride's turbulent shaking, Jim's panicked screams reach my ears, urgently calling my name.

Our carts are on the brink of tipping, and I yell urgently, "Hold on!"

All eyes lock on the front of the roller coaster, and a wave of tension ripples through us. As we descend down the rail, the clicking sound becomes increasingly rapid, creating a sense of exhilaration.

The chase begins as we tip downward with the cart, the shadow losing ground with each passing moment. I can feel the loud and fast thumping in my chest, like a drum beating to an intense rhythm. Dawna's body appears frozen as she stares down at the rail, her hands tightly gripping the front of the cart. The constant growling echoes in my ears, gradually fading with each click.

"As soon as the cart comes to a stop, quickly hop off and sprint toward the gleaming white train without looking behind you," I instruct them.

"Are you sure, Nairb?" Jim asks.

"Yes, I'm sure," I reply loudly.

The sound of the cart's wheels against the straight track fades. Just before we stop, I quickly turn my head and catch a glimpse of the dark shadow swiftly approaching us. The ride comes to a halt, and we climb out. Standing tall, we take a giant step to the right, our bodies swaying slightly as we pull our other leg closer to us. With a determined gaze straight ahead, we start dashing forward, with Dawna's voice commanding, "Make way!"

We repeatedly collide with people, creating a chaotic symphony of apologies and grumbles. The screams of the people behind us echo in the distance. As I briefly turn my head back, I catch a glimpse of the shadow following us.

"Keep going guys. We are almost there. I can see the train," I say, gasping.

We sprint a bit more, turning slightly left when we see the train.

"Run toward the open door," I yell.

The growling seems to be getting closer, its deep rumble vibrating through the surrounding air. Dawna bursts into the train's open cabin, the sound of her hurried footsteps echoing through the air, followed by Jim. The crowd abruptly shifts their attention toward the shadow, their terrified screams piercing the air as they frantically point in my direction. I can hear Jim and Dawna shouting my name and see them vigorously waving their arms at me, their faces flushed and shiny.

As the train doors start sliding in from both sides, the sound of the growl behind me grows louder. I leap toward the opening, my heart pounding in my chest, and catch a glimpse of a shadow reaching out for my right leg as I glance downward.

CHAPTER 11: TRAIN

In the nick of time, a white figure emerges just below my foot, and the shadow's sinister fingers make contact with it. The sound of a deep growl fills the air as I clumsily fall into the small sliding doors, and in an instant, it launches an object from its other hand. As it sails past me, I keep my eyes locked on it, wincing at the clinging sound it makes upon hitting the wall.

With the train in motion, I raise my head and gaze through the windowpane, noticing the scratches and scrapes on the paint. The white figure vanishes, and the shadow immediately gives chase, keeping up with the rapidly accelerating train accompanied by the incessant ticking sound. As I watch, the shadow gradually diminishes in size until it fades away entirely. I glance up at Jim, lifting my right hand in recognition.

Jim's firm grip on my hand pulls me up, concern evident in his voice as he asks if I am alright.

I tell him I'm fine, then scan the concerned faces around me and brush off the dust from my pants.

"Wow, Nairb, that was dangerously close!" Dawna says, her gaze filled with astonishment.

"Yes, it was," I say with a nod, my eyes gleaming with confirmation.

"Where are we going to anyway?" Jim asks, glancing at me as the crowd of people walk away.

"This train will take us downtown Hamilton," I reply, glancing at the window.

"Really?"

"Ya, I didn't know either, but my dad told me long ago; I never actually rode the train before until now. We always took the car."

"Nairb," Dawna looks at me. "Your amulet stopped glowing."

"What do you know, it did," I say, looking down at it. "I guess it glows when the shadow is near."

We are constantly serenaded by the steady clicks from the track filling the train car. Our eyes briefly meet in silence before I shift my gaze to the window, where a captivating sight emerges. The houses on the right mirror the radiant light cascading from above. The fast-moving image outside the open window captivates me, causing my surroundings to blur and darkness to encroach on my periphery. The only thing I can perceive is the vivid image before me, accompanied by the gentle sensation of something repeatedly brushing against my body, causing my hair to sway.

#

"Are you sure about taking this train?" I ask, with a hint of uncertainty.

"Yes," she replies, a gleam in her eyes, "It will be an absolute blast."

"But we don't know where it's going, Grace," I muse, my fingers tapping against my chin in contemplation.

"Does it matter?" Grasping my elbow, she pulls me along, her sense of urgency evident.

"I don't know."

"Come on, let's be adventurous. Don't give me that look, mister."

"Fine."

Stepping onto the blue train, the gentle hum of the engines greets us.

"Grace, we don't have tickets," I whisper, glancing around.

"Don't worry, Nairb, loosen up."

Grasping the white pole at her side, Grace executes a smooth swing around it, her other arm extended in a wide arc. Her hand gracefully twists and turns as she spins, her fingers spread wide open.

"Nairb, look at me."

Looking at her, I whisper, "Grace, please keep calm. People are watching."

"Relax, Nairb. Don't be afraid let them stare." She stands up straight and runs toward the open window on her left.

Her hair gracefully rises, catching the light and creating a mesmerizing glow in her eyes, leaving me unable to look away. I can't help but wonder if she's the one.

"What?" she whispers, her voice barely audible. Is there something on my face?"

Reddening, I quickly respond, "No, no, I was just looking," feeling my forehead glistening with moisture.

"Nairb, how about we check out the other rail car?" she says, jumping off the seat by the open rusty window.

I follow Grace to the connecting door. As I open it for her, a rush of cool air greets us, and it lets out a squeak that echoes like a violin's fading melody, concluding with a soft clap. The moment we enter the room, all eyes turn toward us, creating an uncomfortable silence.

We continue to walk forward, the sound of our footsteps echoing in the quiet.

"Look, Nairb. We can eat there. I see an empty table," she says, turning her head and gesturing toward the inviting spot.

Grace leads the way, and I smell the fragrance of fried chicken in the air. A person greets us from behind a worn brown wooden box, where stacks of papers lay haphazardly.

"Would you like a table?" a gentleman in a black suit asks, gesturing toward the seating area.

"Yes, table for two please," I reply, with Grace standing next to me, her gaze fixed on us as we talk.

"Follow me, please." The server guides us down the aisle, passing the other occupied tables.

"Please sit here," he says, stopping at a table.

Grace sinks into the plush, black-cushioned bench, its glossy surface reflecting the light. I take a seat across from her.

"I'll grab your menus," the server informs us, "Can I get you anything to drink?"

"Yes," I answer softly, "A bottle of red wine, please."
He turns and walks away.
"Wine?" Grace asks.
"Yes, wine. I hope you are okay with that?"
"I am."
The server returns with our menus, delicately placing them on the pristine white tablecloth. Next, he puts a tall, sparkly glass in front of both of us, then presents the label of a unopened red wine bottle; he skillfully unscrews it.

With a gentle tug on the corkscrew end, the cork gradually releases from the top of the bottle. As his face starts to turn a shade of crimson, the cork pops out of the bottle with a sound resembling a balloon popping. He then leans over to my glass, the sound of the wine trickling into my glass filling the air and pours around four tablespoons of wine before leaning back and standing straight, his eyes gazing at me.

With a careful grip, I lift the wine glass, relishing the sensation of the delicate glass against my fingers, and gracefully swirl the wine inside. I lift the glass, and the deep crimson hue of the wine catches my eye as it dances within the glass. As I lower the glass a bit more, it comes to rest against my nose, causing my chest to rise. Bringing the glass to my lips, I can taste the tangy sweetness of the wine as it touches my tongue. As I observe the server with the bottle, I give a subtle nod while lowering my glass.

With a gentle lean towards Grace, he pours the wine into her glass, stopping when it reaches the halfway mark, and then proceeds to pour into mine. Standing upright, he delicately puts the black bottle on the table, ensuring it sits right in the middle.

"I will be back in a moment to take your orders," he says, leisurely strolling away.

"Nairb, I didn't know you were skilled in evaluating the wine's taste," sipping the wine.

"Well, I certainly am. I had to impress you somehow," as I grab the menu.

With a friendly smile, the server comes back and patiently listens as we place our orders. A few minutes later, with our conversation flowing and wine glasses in hand, the server arrives with our plates, and I quickly order another bottle. While enjoying our meal and conversation, I am startled by the sensation of a water droplet sliding down my chest.

Placing my right elbow on the table, I rest my hand against my cheek and direct my gaze toward Grace.

Her eyes lock on mine, her tone laced with curiosity. "What? Is there food in my teeth?"

"No, but you are a bit red," I say, briefly turning my head toward the window and glimpsing the fiery sunset. "Grace, look at the beautiful sunset."

She turns her head to look out the window. "You are right, but can you open the window?"

"Nairb." Jim impatiently taps his foot as he waits for a reply.

With a quick turn of my head, I respond, with watery eyes, "Yes, sorry. I was just thinking about Grace. I miss her."

In a comforting tone, Jim whispers, "Don't worry, it will be alright," and then he pats my back.

"Jim, I think she's keeping a watchful eye on us, making sure we're safe."

"What do you mean?"

"The white figure appears always at the right moment. I think she is here."

"You think?"

"Yes, I don't think those things are coincidental. I believe it's her."

"I really don't know what to say."

"What did you need, anyway?"

"I was wondering if we were almost there?"

I look out both sides of the train, then announce, "Yes, we will stop shortly."

The images through the windows glide past us at a gradual pace before finally freezing as the train halts. The doors slide inside the wall with a squeaky sound, revealing the train station.

Disembarking, Jim leads the way, never releasing Dawna's hand, and I follow closely as we navigate through the crowd. With each passing second, we inch forward, feeling the tight squeeze as we move toward the exit. Like an ant colony marching in unison, everyone scatters in different directions as soon as they step out. As the fresh breeze brushes against my skin, my chest lifts for a moment, and I feel a cool droplet trickle down my back, causing me to squint my eyes.

"We're close to Patty's," I say, "We can just walk there."

Jim turns his head, his eyes scanning the surroundings before confidently stating, "Yes, I know exactly where we are."

We turn right and walk on the light gray sidewalk for a few minutes, the sound of our footsteps echoing in the quiet street. The sound of honking fills the air as a flock of geese flies above us; Jim's right shoulder is splashed with a white object.

He looks at it, a grimace forming on his face. "Does anyone have a tissue?" he asks, hoping to quickly resolve the situation.

"I do," I inform him, reaching into my pocket.

I pass the tissue to him, noticing Dawna's mischievous smirk as she tries to suppress her laughter. With a swift motion, Jim snatches it and begins rubbing the white spot on his shoulder, the sound of his fingers against the fabric filling the air. Dawna and I exchange amused glances, playing along with the seriousness of the moment.

"There," he exclaims, flinging the folded tissue into the green garbage bin next to the withered and stark tree.

We resume our walk, and after a few minutes, the sounds of chirping birds fill the air.

"I can see Patty's house just ahead," Jim says, pointing.

We walk up to the house. "I hope she's home," I say, looking around.

"One way to find out," Jim says, and he and Dawna walk toward the front door.

As we stand on the porch, looking around, ensuring no one is watching us, Jim knocks.

With a steady squeak, the door opens, revealing Patty.

She gestures us in and says, "Come in, come in."

Dawna follows Jim inside. I quickly turn my head to see if anyone is watching us, then enter the house.

Patty closes the door and heads upstairs, saying, "I was expecting you. Let me go get your identifications."

Her footsteps resonate through the hallway, ceasing abruptly before a drawer slides open and closes a few seconds later. As she emerges around a corner, her footsteps echo and grow louder as she moves down the stairs. Each time she descends a step, a clanking noise echoes, like the collision of two wooden boards.

"Here you go," she says, handing us the passports.

"Wow, they look real," I say, flipping through the pages.

"They have to look real; come, sit," Patty exclaims, leading us to the living room.

Jim takes the lead, walking to the gleaming black leather couch, and we quickly plop down, savoring the sensation of its cool surface.

"Can I get you guys something to drink?" Her voice carries a gentle plea, as if she wishes for us to stay longer.

"I'll have a glass of water," I reply, Dawna and Jim following suit.

"Okay, let me go get you some," Patty turns and walks to the kitchen.

Our chests rise in unison as we sigh, almost as if we had rehearsed the motion. Our heads simultaneously turn to each other, our gazes meeting briefly as we exchange nods and raised eyebrows, then return our attentions elsewhere. I shift my gaze to the black scratched wall in front of me, listening to the faint ticking sound emanating from the right. I notice the black handle moving, creating a distinct "tik" sound each time it shifts, tucked away in the corner by the floral lamp on the blue shelf.

Patty returns, handing us glasses of water, and then she sits across from us on the vintage pink leather eighties loveseat.

I twist my head, trying to hide my fascination with the mesmerizing sound that is luring me in. I express my appreciation with a heartfelt thank you.

Patty's eyes shift from left to right, eagerly awaiting the answer to her question. "So, tell me, what exactly did Vlad tell you?"

As I fixate on the pink loveseat she is sitting in, I can't help but marvel at her impeccable sense of design, evident in the harmonious colors surrounding her.

I raise my head, rubbing my temples. "Sorry, I was lost in thought. Can you please repeat your question?"

"No problem," she replies, her curiosity piqued. "So, what did Vlad tell you?"

Locking eyes with Patty, I proceed to inform her of the unfolding events and the exact words that Vlad had spoken. With a nod of understanding, she demonstrates her undivided attention as I continue to delve into explaining what was said and what followed. I don't know if she grasps everything I say, but the furrowed brow on her face speaks volumes.

When I'm done, Patty's eyes shift, concern clear in her gaze. "Jim, are you feeling better now?"

Nodding his head, he reassures her that he is. "Thanks to Nairb," he adds, then takes a sip of water.

"Good," Patty says, rising from her seat. "I'll be right back."

"Wait, where are you going?" Jim asks.

"From what Nairb told me, I gather you guys need a vacation," Patty turns and starts walking away.

Exchanging glances, our eyebrows arch in surprise, followed by a slight shrug of Jim's shoulders.

We sit in silence, occasionally looking in the direction Patty has gone.

She finally returns, saying, "Here you go, guys," and hands a piece of paper to Jim.

Jim looks up and says, "What's this?"

"I figured you guys need some time off, so I got you tickets to get to my cottage."

"Patty, this is unnecessary," Jim says.

"No, it isn't. It's only a short flight from here, and you will be safe from that black thing. We leave for the airport in seven hours."

"I don't know what to say."

"You don't have to say anything; I want to do it," she says, sitting back down on the pink loveseat.

Patty leans closer, her voice filled with excitement as she describes the picturesque location and then provides detailed directions to her cottage from the plane.

"Patty?"

She looks at me. "Yes, Nairb?"

"Can I borrow your car for an hour?"

"Why?"

"I want to see my house."

"Nairb, that is not a good idea," Jim states.

"We can't stop his urge to go and see his house. When your amulet turns blue, level immediately." Dawna says.

"I will."

"Here are the keys. Just return soon," Patty says, grabbing them from the side pocket of her black pants.

I take the keys, thank her, and head for the door.

"Just there and back."

Opening the door, I quickly look back and see the anxious expressions on Jim and Dawna's faces. As I turn my head back, I smile and step outside feeling the warm breeze brushing against my face. As I gaze at Patty's white car to the right of me, just a few meters away.

I walk to the white car, unlock the driver's side door, and sink into the plush, black leather seat, savoring its softness. The sound of the engine starting echoes in my ears, accompanied by the pungent smell of gasoline. I glance at the rearview mirror, catching a glimpse of the darkness behind me, before quickly readjusting it. With my final check, I put the car in gear and slowly roll forward, noticing a small dark white cloud trailing behind me in the side mirror. I turned onto the road, and just moments later, the engine roars like a mighty lion, creating an exhilarating atmosphere.

Thoughts race through my mind as I drive, a mix of anticipation, causing my chest to pound and moisture to well up in my eyes. Turning left onto my street, I catch a glimpse of my reflection in the mirror and quickly run and wipe my eyes. Driving forward, I spot a charred tree on my left, while fresh green stems emerge and reach for the sky. As I drive closer to my house, I notice bright yellow tape encircling it, cautioning everyone to stay away.

I fix my gaze on the black wood, of the house and shut off the engine I rest my forehead against the window, my eyes growing misty. With my teeth clenched, I push open the door and step out, my footsteps echoing as I approach the tape. I tilt my head and scan the area, moving my gaze from left to right. I lift the tape up and walk under it, the sound of crinkling plastic filling the air as I make my way forward on the driveway toward a burned car. Its hood remains raised, revealing the charred engine beneath.

I hear the crunch of ash and debris under my shoes as I make my way up the burned piles of dirt and wood. I noticed a flicker of something shiny reflecting the light and bouncing away. With every step I take toward it, I hear the crunch of leaves and twigs beneath my feet. Bending down, I notice the faint scent of old paper emanating from the small picture frame. Using my right-hand fingers, I gently brush away the black dust that has accumulated on it. I fix my eyes on the frame, and a minuscule drop lands on it, gliding along the surface and landing on Grace's outstretched arm, where she cradles a bear won at a fair on our date.

The sound of more drops falling accompanies my discovery of the mesmerizing blue light on my amulet, prompting me to sway my head from side to side. I eagerly gaze ahead as an object rises from the rubble just a few meters across from me, the sound of sliding burned wood and crashing objects filling the air. The sound of crunching draws nearer, bloodshot eyes stare, and a growl produces a cloud of dust, causing my chest to slow and droplets to form under my shirt. I drop the picture frame.

CHAPTER 12: RUN

I feel a shiver run down my spine as goosebumps prickle all over my body. A cloud of dust coats me from head to toe. With a quick glance to either side, I pause momentarily before dashing off to the right. I feel my heart pounding against my ribcage, its rhythm quick and erratic. I hear the deep, rhythmic sound of air being sucked in with every step, accompanied by the crouching sound and crackling beneath my feet. The sight of a parked car by the curb catches my eye, while a loud growl resonates in the distance, making me uneasy. Meanwhile, my amulet glows even brighter blue as if it wants to convey a message.

I enter the car, my hand trembling, and slam the door shut behind me. After three attempts, I finally manage to insert the key into the keyhole. When I turn my head to the right, I am met with the unsettling sight of bloodshot eyes staring directly at me. In response, I stomp on the gas pedal, causing the tires to squeal. Looking in the rearview mirror, I see it receding into the distance. The engine roars and the black glow gradually fades away, leaving behind a calming silence.

As I peer into the review mirror, my face reflects a shade of crimson, prompting me to swiftly wipe my forehead with my left forearm. I then refocus my attention ahead, relishing the sensation of the wind caressing my face. After a minute, I make a right turn and am instantly drawn to the radiant light rays reflecting off the vibrant glass images, with peculiar objects hovering above certain ones.

I guide my car to the right, signaling my intention, and come to a halt beside a sleek, black vehicle. The noise slowly fades away, leaving behind a cloud of brown dust that twirls around me as I open my door. The sound of birds tweeting above catches my attention, and as I look up, I witness a flock of white birds gracefully gliding through the sky, then vanish from sight.

A bird catches my attention, sitting atop a smooth, gray rock, its presence seemingly indicating the direction I am headed. With each passing moment, my heart beats faster and I feel a warm sensation inside me. As I glance down at my arm, I notice all the tiny hairs standing on end, guiding me in the right direction. I come to a halt and slowly turn my head from left to right, mustering up a firm, resounding voice as I call out Grace's name.

Holding my breath, I move my head from side to side, my eyes scanning the area, but the only sound that reaches my ears is a car driving by on the distant road. A minute passes, and my chest rises as I release my breath, then turn around, keeping my head down. As I take a step, I feel a gentle poke on my right shoulder, as if someone is silently urging me to look their way.

I turn my head and see Grace, with a glowing white around her. "Grace, it's you! I can see you!" I exclaim.

"Yes, it's me."

"How do you know it's me?" she asks.

"Your voice gives it away."

"There are so many questions I want to ask you. I love you; I need you." Grace's touch on my cheek instantly spreads warmth through my skin, moisturizing my eyes.

"I know; I love you too; I was always by your side."

"The bright light, was you?"

"Yes, there are so many things I wish to tell you, but I can't." Grace lowers her hand, her fingers grazing against the soft fabric of her dress.

"Do you know why that strange thing is after me, and what about these powers?"

"Indeed, it has fled and made its way to this location. Your powers beckon it, craving to assimilate them. Just lure it here, and I will deal with it."

"Why did I get these gifts, and why did you leave me?"

"You have been chosen, and I never left you. I'm always in your heart." Grace taps my chest. "It is the main reason you are seeing me."

"Grace, I don't want this; I just want you back." I feel tears flow down my cheeks.

As she approaches me, her fingers reach out and delicately wipe my cheeks, and I see her eyes shimmer with reflection.

"There are things we cannot change. I love you, and I want to let you know that."

"I couldn't save you," I lament, my heart heavy with guilt, and I drop to my knees beside the dark spots of my tears.

Grace's comforting touch on my shoulder accompanies her words. "You mustn't blame yourself. It wasn't your fault; it was simply meant to happen."

"I need your guidance," I say, my voice filled with desperation.

"You'll be okay. Time is running out. Just remember to bring it here."

In a blink, Grace disappears, and I cry out for her.

Scanning the area with my eyes, I hear a bird tweeting from a faraway tree that appears to be newly planted.

With my head down, I return to the car, feeling a constant tingling sensation on my cheeks, like a gentle feather gliding downward. As I open the door and step inside, I slam it shut behind me, my heart pounding in my chest.

Gazing out the window, I watch the leaves swaying from side to side on a tree, catching me in a hypnotic-like trance.

#

"Nairb, are you sure this is the right place for a swing?" she inquires, looking around at the lack of sturdy branches.

"I'm certain," I affirm. This tree is solid." I place the white rope and small yellow wooden board on the ground.

"Okay, just be careful," she cautions, her voice tinged with concern. "I don't want you to get a painful splinter or a nasty scrape."

"Don't worry," I say, climbing the tree with the rope. With a swift motion, I tie the rope around the light black branch and declare that I am done.

As I descend the tree, I jump off midway and gracefully land on the newly cut grass. I walk up to the hanging rope and grab its end. After mounting the board on the rope, I sit on it, feeling the rough texture beneath me. I push off, raising my legs and hopping off after a few seconds.

Walking over to Grace, I gesture toward the swing and say, "Look, there it is. I told you I could do it."

Grace does a double take, her eyes widening, before dashing over to it. As she pushes off with her feet, the sound of the thick rope sliding against the branch fills the yard.

With her luminous hair dancing in the air, she smiles at me and exclaims, "You were absolutely right, this is fantastic!"

Looking up, I quickly wipe my eyes with my hands, then glance down to turn the keys in the ignition, the engine's rumble echoing in my ears. I put the car in gear, and the sight of a dense cloud of brown dust swirling behind me fills my rearview mirror.

Driving straight, I take a moment to appreciate the refreshing scent of the air as I breathe deeply, then lift my foot off the gas pedal. Through the window, the images outside slide by leisurely, revealing glimpses of lush green trees and bushes emerging from a hazy blur. With a firm press on the brake pedal, a piercing squeak echoes through the air, while a thick cloud of white smoke engulfs the surroundings. As I gaze forward, my knuckles turn white, the car's gentle vibrations coursing through my hands. With a squeak, the vehicle sharply turns around, causing a slight tilt, and the sound of it bounces off the green trees as if they are mimicking the noise.

I move forward, the engine purring like a contented cat, and roll the window down to hear the sounds. My thoughts stop as a gust of wind sweep through, causing my hair to sway. I clearly understand what needs to be done, so I turn in Patty's direction.

Stepping out of the car, I am greeted by the sound of birds chirping and the scent of freshly cut grass in Patty's driveway. I walk up to the door, push it open, and step inside.

Everyone turns to look at me, exclaiming, "You're back!"

Closing the door behind me, I nod, then walk to the couch, sinking into its soft cushions.

"Did everything go smoothly?" Patty asks.

"Yes, everything is good," I answer, feeling Jim's reassuring pat on my right thigh.

No one asks me further questions; their knowing expressions speak volumes. Dawna and Jim lean back on the couch, their bodies sinking into its worn-out grooves.

"Before we go," Patty suggests, glancing at her wrist, "Do you guys want something to eat?"

Like a synchronized symphony, we all look at each other to ensure everyone agrees, then simultaneously shake our heads.

"All right then, we should go," Patty says, her fingers crossed in anticipation.

As we get up from the couch, we fall in line behind Patty, with Jim at the front and me at the back. Patty holds the door open, allowing us to exit, and each of us raises our head in gratitude.

She closes the door behind her, the sound of its latch echoing through the empty house.

We follow Patty to her car, its sleek exterior reflecting the light.

"The car looks good, Nairb," Patty says, running her fingers along the smooth surface as she opens her door.

I don't reply, instead answering with a silent gaze.

Jim and I hop in the back seat.

As Dawna settles into the passenger seat, she turns to Patty and says, "Thank you for this."

"Yes, thank you," Jim agrees.

I remain silent, lost in contemplation of what has transpired, debating whether to reveal it. Instead, I find solace in wrapping my finger around the delicate amulet.

"How far from the airport is the cottage?" Dawna inquires.

"It's just a short distance, maybe a thirty-minute drive."

I glimpse Patty's pleading eyes in the rearview mirror, as if she desires something.

"Listen, guys." Patty begins.

As she explains what to do once we land, we all nod in agreement. After finishing her speech, we drive in silence.

Upon arriving at the airport, Patty turns the engine off, hands the cottage keys to Jim, and the three of us get out of the car, gently closing our door behind us.

Opening her window, she reminds us of what we are to do, and we nod, then thank her for everything, waving as she drives away.

After a few seconds, we look at each other, our eyes meeting, before making our way toward the departing booth through the sliding glass door. The petite women, with her keen eyes, verify our names on our passports and then indicate the way to the plane. We wait a few minutes in the dimly lit lobby, its gray walls giving off a somber ambiance. The row of seats is already occupied with other weary travelers. As the lady beckons for people to enter, the sound of shuffling feet fills the room, and the brown seats are soon deserted. Jim goes through the checkpoint first, then waits for us a few meters away. I show the lady my ticket and passport, and her gaze lingers on me for a few seconds, before she finally lets me through. Dawna's face pales with each passing second as she waits for her turn, and her hands shake uncontrollably, dropping her passport.

PLANE

Squatting down, Dawna picked up her passport, feeling the weight of it in her hand. Dawna's face was moist and shimmering as she stood up while the lady swiftly moved to the next person in line. As we gazed at her every move, Dawna walked up to us with a confident stride.

"That was close," Dawna whispers, her face moist.

"Yes, it was," I reply.

Jim nudges my stomach, directing my attention to the

four wheelchair-bound individuals being gently guided toward the plane door. We stand by, watching as they roll past us, their wheels squeaking.

I turn my head to Jim and exchange a playful wink, planning something in my mind.

A voice over a loudspeaker starts to call out row numbers, and when ours is called, we get in line to board the plane.

Finally, we find ourselves sinking into our seats, our knees brushing against the smooth gray plastic. Dawna's gaze is fixed out the window, occasionally breaking into a smile as the pilot's voice echoes through the speakers hanging from the ceiling.

Once in the air, I tap Jim's thigh and take in the panoramic view from above.

After we are told we can take off our seatbelts, I stand up.

"Where do you think you're headed?" Jim asks, while Dawna turns her head in my direction.

I quietly respond, "To find those people in the wheelchairs."

"I don't think that is a good idea," Jim whispers, his words barely audible.

"Don't worry, I say firmly, my words carrying a sense of determination and confidence. I have a well-thought-out plan. I will be back soon." I tap the top of my seat with my hand, feeling its smooth surface, and start strolling to the right.

I walk up the aisle to the front, then push the brown curtains open. A cloud of gray particles cascades down, creating a misty atmosphere. I hurriedly tousle my hair and adjust my posture, swiveling my head left and right.

On both sides of the walkway, I notice wheelchairs, their frames secured by a sleek black belt and resting on what appears to be black metal. I meander toward them and come to a stop in front of one.

"If you don't mind me asking, what happened to you guys?" I ask.

"We were in a bobsled accident. Why?" he replies.

I look around, the sound of hushed voices and distant footsteps echoing through the plane.

"I will help you guys, but you can't say a word about this." Everyone nods.

I turn my head in both directions, taking in the view around, and then walk up to the curtains and slide them closed.

With speed, I reach the closest person and urgently demand them to give me their right arm.

He stretches it out, and as I firmly grasp it, I sense a powerful surge of energy flowing from me. Three more times, I repeat this process, turning around and finishing it. After doing this four times, I feel a strong wave of dizziness, almost resembling the sensation of being intoxicated. I drop to my knees, the sound of my heavy breaths filling the silence.

"Are you feeling alright, sir?"

Closing my eyes briefly, I take a deep breath and reassure myself, "Yes, I'm okay," before standing up and walking toward the curtain.

As I slide back the curtains, I remind them of our secret agreement, my eyes darting to each of them.

"You have our word," one of the men replies, their synchronized head movements signaling their unanimous agreement. "And thank you!"

I smile as I drop to one knee and stand up, feeling unsteady.

I make it back to my seat and plop down crookedly, the force causing a slight bounce.

Jim turns his head, his eyebrows furrowing as he asks, "You look pale."

"I think I healed the individuals in the wheelchairs," I told him, readjusting in my seat.

"Are you serious?"

"Yes!"

"No one saw you, I hope."

"Nobody saw me."

"Good. Did it work?"

"Let's just say we will know in a few hours."

"I think this is great, Nairb," Dawna says, leaning forward.

"Thank you. Now, I'm sorry, you two, but I must close my eyes."

"No problem. You look exhausted," Jim informs me.

"Just wake me up once we land," I say, putting a pillow behind my head.

"We will. Go to sleep," Dawna says, turning off the bright light above my head.

As I doze, Grace keeps appearing and disappearing every time she wants to say something to me. I see a cabin in the dark woods, with smoke coming out of a chimney. I hear a bird tweeting in a tree nearby, and there's the smell of colorful flowers all around me. It makes me feel all warm and fuzzy to see Grace hanging white sheets on a clothesline outside the cabin. When she looks in my direction, everything goes dark. I'm screaming, but it's dead silent and pitch dark. I'm constantly turning my head and body. I can hear a fast-knocking sound as I struggle to catch my breath, and I see bloodshot eyes in the dark in front of me. I scream and swing, hearing my name called repeatedly, its volume increasing. The ground beneath me trembles as the bloody eyes in the distance draw nearer, causing me to let out a blood-curdling scream, and then I see Jim.

"You had a nightmare," he says.

I turn my head left and right and see that I am on the plane, with Jim and Dawna beside me.

Feeling warm and sweaty, I readjust myself in the seat.

"We are about to land," Jim announces, and I can feel the plane descending.

"How long was I out?"

"One or two hours."

"Seriously, that much time has passed?"

"Yes, we would have let you sleep until we landed, but you started swinging, and Dawna insisted we wake you up. What did you dream of?"

"I saw Grace, then the shadow was after me."

"I see. Good thing we woke you up then." Just then, a voice comes over the speakers, instructing everyone to sit and put on our seatbelts for landing.

As the plane touches down, the vibrations resonate through our seats and reverberate through our bodies. The shaking noise echoes through the air, resembling the grating of rubber on rubber, and I tightly clench my seat, digging my nails into the fabric.

When it is time to disembark, I stand up and gingerly move down the aisle, trying not to bump into the people ahead of us; Jim and Dawna follow slowly behind me.

As we walk into the lobby, the air is filled with the cacophony of screams, instantly capturing everyone's attention.

CHAPTER 13: ESCAPE

As we turn our heads to the left, we catch sight of someone leaping in the air, an empty wheelchair behind them.

"I guess it worked," I say with a mischievous grin.

I quickly glance at Jim and Dawna, their presence beside me adding a sense of camaraderie as we make our way to the glass sliding exit door.

"Hey, Jim, do the directions tell us to take a left or right turn once we're outside?" I inquire.

"We go left, Patty said, then there are taxies there."

Making our way through the sliding door, we take a left turn onto the gray sidewalk, where a black pole gleams bright white just a few meters overhead. The sight of yellow cars lined up in a neat row is accompanied by the sound of the first one's engine purring. Opening the door cautiously, I lean my head inside and feel the chill of the hood against my left arm. That's when I hear the command to get in. Dawna and Jim slip inside, the door closing behind them with a silent squeak, just like mine.

I inform the driver about the directions we have been given, and we begin to drive away, the landscape slowly shifting as we leave the airport. While my eyes scan the area, I notice a tape player with faded black dials and hear a radio playing classical music, and emitting a soft, green glow. I turn to face my friends, and I notice they are moving their heads up and down to the music. Briefly turning his head, Jim makes eye contact with me, flashing a playful grin.

With a gradual increase in speed, we begin to spot other cars in various vibrant hues along the road. As I scratch my itchy leg, I notice the vibrant blue light radiating from my amulet. Instantly, my eyes grow wide, and I quickly turn my body and head in all directions before finally stopping at Jim.

"Jim, Dawna, we have a problem," I exclaim, pointing urgently at my amulet.

Their gazes drop to the amulet.

"There is something black flying up there," the driver announces, looking in the rearview mirror.

"Step on it," I shout.

The powerful roar of the engine surrounds us as our bodies sway with the speed, a stream of black smoke in the back.

"What is that?" the driver yells, squinting his eyes to get a better look.

I quickly glance at the dashboard and see the needle pointing at fifty.

"Go faster!" I order.

"I can't go any faster," he says, the needle on the speed-ometer gliding from left to right.

"My eighty-year-old grandma can drive faster than this," I shout.

As a loud bang echoes through the air, our heads instinctively turn upward.

"Get down," I holler.

The hand, dark as night, has fingers that resemble sharp, thick razor blades, mercilessly cutting through anything in its way, moving in unpredictable directions.

The driver yells, "Hang on," and our bodies move from side to side.

The hand's disappearance coincides with the alarming sound of knocking and banging on the roof of the car.

With a determined effort, Dawna lifts herself from the floor, sweeping away the glass that covers the shredded seat. Her teeth clench together, their white brilliance starkly contrasting with the wreckage before her.

As our bodies bounce around, we hear the jarring sound of a loud scrape overhead, and everything falls silent.

Dawna points and shouts, her hair standing on end, "Look, it's after us again!"

"Hang on," the driver shout, the smell of dust and gravel filling the air as he aggressively turns the steering wheel to the right and onto the gravel road.

With our bodies tilted to the left, we turned our heads and catch sight of its menacing, bloodshot eyes and its sharp, reaching hands.

The sound of Jim's excited voice fills the air as he shouts, "Look over there! Something white is flying toward it at lightning speed," prompting me to turn my head.

I watch attentively, knowing it's Grace, and quietly say, "Thank you, Grace."

"What did you say?" Jim asks loudly.

The shattered window makes it difficult to make out my words. "I said that thing," I respond, with my hair raising.

A blinding flash of light illuminates our surroundings, followed by a booming thunder that makes us each of us turn our head.

The sight of Grace and the shadow moving their hands captivates us, their gestures shrinking until they vanish, and then we turn our bodies around. The overwhelming vibrations gradually fade into the background, leaving behind only the gentle touch of a subtle whistle dancing across my face and gently lifting my hair.

As the taxi lessens its speed, I turn my head in confusion and ask, "Why are you slowing down?"

"The car just shut off," the driver responds, frustration evident in the repetitive clicking of the key knob.

Dawna leans forward, her eyebrows furrowing in confusion. "What is happening? Why are we suddenly slowing down?"

"Great, it looks like we are having car issues," I say.

Dawna briefly glances at Jim, then leans back and resumes gazing out of the shattered open window, her hair swaying gently with each movement. We stop, our eyes locking for a brief moment, silently communicating.

"Let's see what the problem is," the driver says, his fingers grasping the door handle with a sense of urgency.

We all get out of the car, the grinding of gravel beneath our feet adding to the ambiance. Standing shoulder to shoulder, we form a tight cluster, resembling a team huddle, our eyes focused downward.

"Let's investigate," the driver exclaims, lifting the hood.

As he raises his hand, a billowing cloud of white-hot smoke erupts with a sizzling sound, causing the driver to scream.

"What's wrong?" I shout.

He waved his hands near his face and says, "The car has overheated, so we're stuck here."

As I gaze down at the white smoke, accompanied by the sizzling sound, I briefly glance at Jim and Dawna, their noses crinkling at the pungent aroma.

"Great!" I exclaim, my voice dripping with sarcasm.

"Do you have any idea how much farther we have to go?" I inquire, my breath coming in brief gasps.

"You are up the road, maybe a few minutes from here."

"Really!" I respond excitedly, glancing at Jim and Dawna.

"Yes," the driver says, pointing at the bright light in the distance. "You can just walk there. You guys go. I'll be fine."

"Okay, great," I say, reaching into my pocket. "How much do I owe you?"

"Don't worry about paying for the exciting adventure. You guys go."

"Thank you," we say and start walking the direction he has directed us.

As our footsteps create a crackling sound on the gravel beneath our feet, Grace occupies my thoughts, and a multitude of questions race through my mind about her well-being and what might have happened to her.

I look back, noticing the white smoke still rising from the taxi.

Dawna's face lights up with excitement and she screams, "This is the cottage!" pointing to the left.

We turned our heads. "You think?" Jim asks.

"Yes, it has that prominent gray rock Patty told us about, and a tall tree standing in harmony with it."

"Yes, I think you're right. What do you think, Nairb?"

"I think she is right, Jim."

As we turn left, the green bushes part to reveal a log cottage, its brown wood blending seamlessly with the surrounding nature. When we reach the front door, Jim glances downward and wrestles with his pant pocket. With a firm grip on the circular gold handle, he inserts the key into the lock and turns it, hearing the satisfying click. The moment he pushes the brown wooden door open, we are plunged into an abyss of pitch darkness.

"She said there is a light switch on your right. Flick it," Dawna instructs.

With a swift motion, Jim turns his head and flicks the light switch, instantly flooding the room with brightness.

"Wow, this is what I'm talking about," I say, walking farther into the room.

"Jim, this place is luxurious. Look at all that stuff."

"I never knew Patty was so well off," Jim says, sitting on the shiny black leather couch.

"Look!" Dawna shout, her eyes widening at the breathtaking view before her. "Jim, you won't believe it, but this washroom is as big as our master bedroom."

As Jim approaches his wife, he squints his eyes against the blinding sparkles and quickly walks away.

"Look at that pristine white carpet, perfectly complemented by the fireplace's warm glow," I say.

Jim turns, a look of wonder setting in his face. "That's a white bear!"

As if by magic, a crack materializes in front of the TV, allowing Patty's room to be seen through the shimmering fracture.

"Nairb, I thought you had lost that remarkable ability?"

"I thought I did," I reply, my thoughts consumed about Patty. "Should we go to Patty's house?"

"Feel free to go ahead without me. I need to take a shower. I noticed some clothes over there." Dawna says.

As our heads turn in unison, Jim and I lock eyes, silently communicating our readiness to go and get our instructions.

"Shall we, Jim?"

He approaches the crack, his eyes meeting mine, before he diverts his gaze toward Patty's room, taking a moment to assess the surroundings, and then disappears inside. I make my way through the crack and find myself standing beside Jim. We watch as the white rays of light shift and swirl. The calming, hypnotizing buzzing sound fills the air as room at Patty's cottage starts to shrink, making a popping sound as it disappears.

As a figure approaches us, I look forward and feel a rush of warmth.

CHAPTER 14: SURPRISED

As the person gets closer to us, we see it is Patty. "Oh, it's you," Jim says.

"Of course, it's me," Patty replies, her voice tinged with a mix of familiarity and exasperation. "Who else would it be? I live here. How did you guys get here anyway? Wait, where is Dawna?"

"She is taking a shower at your cabin."

"My cabin?" she asks, her voice echoing through the empty room.

"Yes, your cabin. Nairb can open a crack to the cabin."

"A crack?"

"That's what we call it. It's basically a portal. Nairb can do it again so that we can go back there."

"Really!" she exclaims, with wide-eyed astonishment. "Is this true? You can open a portal to places?"

"Yes, it's true. I just got my ability back. You are my first test."

"And you can go anywhere?"

"Pretty much, but I have to imagine the place to open the crack, like looking at a picture and imagine myself there."

"Patty, do you want to go to your cabin now?"

She is silent for a minute, thinking, and then says she would.

I focus on the moment at Patty's cottage when Jim and I stood side by side, marveling at the sight of my crack; it appears out of nowhere, accompanied by a humming sound that reverberates through the air. As the light dances in the crack, it reveals a captivating image of the imagined place. Looking through the formation of the crack, it is as if we are peering into a different place altogether.

With her hand shielding her eyes, Patty asks, "Will this lead me to my cabin?"

"Yes, it will."

"And is this safe walking through?"

"Yes, it's safe. Just do it. We will be right behind you."

As Patty turns her head toward me, I catch a glimpse of her determined expression before she closes her eyes and steps through. With a brief look at Jim, I turn my gaze back to her, and Jim follows suit, trailing behind me as we move forward.

The moment we enter the cottage, it feels as though we have seamlessly transitioned into the next room. Patty's gaze fixates on us, almost as if she needs reassurance that we have truly arrived.

"Wow, Nairb, your gift is incredible," Patty says, her head turning in all directions as she takes in the sights of the place.

"Thanks," I say, approaching the cozy couch.

"Patty, how did you secure this incredible location?"

"My grandparents left this for me; what is that sound?" In accord, our heads swivel to glimpse what is causing the commotion.

"That sound," Jim answers, "is Dawna's blissful shower."

"Patty, are we protected here from the relentless pursuit of that shadow?" I ask in a soft voice.

"See that blue crystal with sharp corners on that brown wooden stand?" Patty points.

"Yes."

"Just like your amulet, but on a much grander scale, the crystal functions as both a shield and a repellent, rendering it impenetrable. Your amulet functions as a warning signal, alerting you to its presence but lacking the force to deter it."

"Okay, that's good to know."

Just then, Dawna comes out with a towel on her head.

"Patty, you're here. I'm sorry I'm not appropriately dressed."

"No need to worry. I was actually on my way out. Nairb was simply showing his knack for navigation. Please make yourself comfortable, as if you were at home. Oh, look, I see a star," she adds, turning her head towards me and staring wide-eyed momentarily.

As soon as Patty and I exchange glances, a crack emerges a few meters in front of her, causing her hair and clothes to glow.

"It's time for me to go," Patty says with a sigh, turning and stepping into the crack.

She turns around and waves at us, and we wave back enthusiastically.

"Bye," Dawna says loudly, her voice carrying over the distance. "And thank you."

Our gazes fixate on Patty as she vanishes from our view, leaving us with a sense of emptiness.

"I'm going to shower next," Jim says and kisses Dawna on the cheek.

"I'll see what there is to make us for supper" she says, walking toward the silver fridge.

"Thank you, Dawna, but it's unnecessary."

With a playful smile, she said, "Oh, Nairb, you're being silly. I'll make something, I'm not the best cook but will how it will turn out," she said, turning her head and opening the fridge.

I stroll over to a white fluffy couch in front of the TV. As I plop onto it, I am embraced by the gentle lift and sinking sensation of the cushions, which provide me with instant comfort.

As I settled in, I leisurely extend my left arm behind my head, and with a quick reach to my right, I grab the remote.

Mindlessly surfing through the channels, I accidentally tune into the news and catch a fleeting glimpse of my reflection. With the volume raised, a vivid picture of us appears before my eyes.

"Dawna, quickly look," I shout, my voice filled with urgency.

"Crank up the volume. I can barely hear anything."

I turn it up, and Dawna watches intently with me. The news lady's voice grows grave as she informs the public about our status as fugitives. She urges everyone to keep an eye out for us and call the police without hesitation if we are seen.

Dawna's skin takes on a reddish tint as she ordered, "Turn off the TV; supper is ready," before walking briskly towards the table.

By pressing the red button on the remote, I stand up from the couch and drop the remote before making my way to the kitchen table.

"What did I miss?" Jim pops out, his sudden appearance startling us.

He vigorously rubbed the pink towel on his head.

"Nothing, Jim. Make your way to the kitchen table; we're about to indulge in a delicious meal. Dawna made something for us."

Jim and I make our way to the table, Jim's disheveled hair still being tousled as he walks. As we both take a seat, Dawna positions a jar of red jam and some buns on an empty plate in the middle of the table and then settles down to my right.

"I found these. There wasn't much in the fridge. I couldn't find much else," Dawna said, her eyes moving side to side.

Jim picks up a bun and taps it with his finger, producing a resonant sound that fills the surrounding air.

"Don't give me that look. It's what I found. I guess we need to do some grocery shopping. The fridge was practically empty," Dawna said and bit the bun.

Jim's eyes briefly meet mine, but it's the bun that captures his full attention. After spreading jam on it, he gazes at it, his anticipation evident, before finally taking a bite. Not wanting to miss out, I quickly follow his lead. Our eyes lock onto each other's gaze while we chew.

"So, is it okay?" Dawna says, reaching for the jar.

"Yes," Jim responds, the sound of his chewing punctuating his words.

"Shh," Dawna says softly.

"What?"

"Quiet," she whispers, straining her ears for any sound.

"I apologize if my chewing was loud," Jim chuckles, aware that it may have been noticeable.

Dawna rolls her eyes at him.

"There it is again," Dawna says, her eyes scanning the surroundings for any sign of movement.

The silence in the cottage is shattered by a single, powerful thump that bellows through the entire space.

Dawna and I glance down, our eyes widening as we notice my amulet is emanating a brilliant, luminous blue glow.

"Look," Jim points excitedly, "That crystal is glowing too!"

The windows tremble from the force of a menacing growl that echoes through the room, leaving us all frozen in place, exchanging worried looks.

"Shall we run?" Dawna asks, her complexion drained of color, a worried expression on her face.

"No, I don't think so. Patty said we are okay here," Jim answers, his mouth full as he takes another bite.

Another thump resounds, accompanied by a menacing growl, as the crystal light fills the room with a brilliant, intense blue glow. Following the sound of a distant whistle coming from under the door, a quiet calm settles in, gradually replacing the fleeting noise.

We all look at one another. "Just ignore it," Jim tells us.

We do as he says, then continue biting into our buns.

"Nairb, I'm going to go lie down in the bedroom for a bit. That flight drained me." Dawna exclaims.

"I will join you," Jim says.

"I'm just going to watch some TV. I'm not really tired; this time change has not been adopted yet. Besides, I slept on the plane."

"Okay," Dawna says, gazing my way.

We stand up, and I head toward the cozy, fluffy white couch, while Jim and Dawna leisurely walk to the bedroom, passing the washroom, and disappearing into a room on the left.

As I reach out and grab the remote, I can feel its weight in my hand, and with precision, I point it at the screen and press the red button, the soft sound of the click filling the air. As I flip through the channels, my eyes are drawn to a captivating cartoon that I can't help but stop and gaze at. As I settle into the cushions, I kick my feet up on the end and let my left arm drape behind my head. From this relaxed position, I watch the animated program, occasionally breaking into a smile. After a while, my feet touch the ground, and I finally press the off button. Its satisfying click echoes in the room as I turn my head toward the window, curious about what I will see. The scene before me is shrouded in darkness, except for a lone tree swaying gently, its leaves rustling and creating a mesmerizing display.

A few minutes pass, and then I turn my head and gaze forward, until a captivating glow of moving light appears before my eyes.

As I stand on the grass, I marveled the vibrant colors of the surrounding trees, each one more beautiful than the last. When I look down, I discover a large, smooth rock, its gray surface inviting me to take a seat. I fixate on the rock in front of me, gradually losing focus as my eyes grow blurry. I rub them, then continue to gaze, taking in the scent with each sniff.

#

The flames grow higher with each log I place on the fire, and the warmth spreads throughout.

"Nairb, the fire is fine," Grace says, patting the log invitingly.

"Okay, okay, I'm coming," I tell her, hastily standing up and leaving the brown steel rod behind.

The red ashes swirl around us, and one of the fiery flakes lands softly on the back of my neck as my hair dances in the wind. With a quick swat, I start running and jumping, with a burst of determination.

"What are you doing?" she asks, raising an eyebrow.

"The ash fell on the back of my neck."

"Are you alright?"

"Yes," I say, walking toward her, holding my neck.

By my side, Grace soothes me by rubbing my back.

"Better?"

"Yes," I respond.

"Here is your stick," Grace says, extending it toward me with a smile. As I hold it, I can feel the weight of its longstanding history and the familiar, worn texture that has been shaped by countless hands before mine.

While we roast together, I notice her reddish cheeks, illuminated by the shifting orange light.

"Nairb, isn't it amazing how we can leave everything behind and rely on the moon to guide us through? Plus, the clear night sky allows us to see countless stars," Grace says, gazing at the sky.

I look up, I say, "Yes, but the constant buzzing of mosquitos is not really my thing."

"A little buzz, a little prick here and there, just breathe, Nairb, just breathe in deep."

The forest is alive with the scent of pine and earth, creating a refreshing aroma as Grace explores. She takes a deep breath, savoring the crisp, fresh air.

"More like lots of buzzing and lots of pricking."

"Just breathe and close your eyes." Grace takes a deep breath, shutting her eyes and blocking out the world around her.

Her smile captivates me, causing me to turn my head and close my eyes, immersing myself in the blissful feeling.

"Do you hear that?"

"What is it you want me to hear? I just hear crickets."

"That is nature, Nairb."

"Yes, nothing but nature and the sound of the mosquitoes."

"Nairb, hurry! Look up!" she exclaims, pointing up at the flying star.

I open my eyes and briefly look up." There's no need, Grace; I already have my wish."

Grace's cheeks turn crimson.

As I walk toward the light, I eagerly wipe my eyes and let out a contented sigh.

I rub my eyes again, slowly walking toward the couch. I sink into its soft cushions and gaze out as the lush green grass and fallen branches gradually fade from my view. My eyes then drift over to the bookshelf, filled to the brim, and I find myself lost in Grace's captivating presence for a few more blissful minutes.

The distant sound of gentle footsteps reaches my ears, and as I turn my head, I see Jim standing in his boxers.

"Are you doing okay, buddy?" He asks, walking over and sitting down beside me.

"Yes, my mind was just reflecting."

"Were you thinking about Grace?"

"Yes, and the things she said to me earlier, like that the light is her."

"Are you serious?"

With blurry vision, I turned my head and replied, "Yes."

I mentioned the events that took place and Grace's words. Whether he believed me in that moment remained unclear, but his presence emitted a sense of trust.

"Don't worry," Jim says soothingly, patting my back for reassurance.

"Thanks," I acknowledge, then add, "Hey, we should go touch base with Connie."

"Wait, I need to go put on some clothes," he says, getting up and heading to the bedroom.

He comes out a few seconds later, hopping on one leg, putting on his pants as he moves toward me.

"What about Dawna?" I inquire.

"She's sleeping. There's no need to wake her; let her sleep."

Jim stands beside me, his excited energy palpable.

"You ready?" I ask, my eyes gleaming with anticipation.

He nods, and we start to walk toward the increasing brightness that floods the room.

"This is the place," Jim says, seeing some familiar objects in Connie's house.

"Good," I reply, and we go through the crack.

"I hear footsteps," Jim whispers.

"Connie?" I call, my eyes scanning the room.

"What are you doing in my house?" Connie's voice startles us as she appears before us, her eyes wide.

"How did you get in?" Her eyes dart back and forth between Jim and I, and she threatens to call the police.

"There is no need for the police," I say. "It's me, Nairb, and that's Jim."

"Prove it," she challenges skeptically, crossing her arms.

Pointing to his knuckle, Jim reveals the lasting evidence of his fierce punch, a bruise that serves as a reminder of their previous successful escape.

"Nairb, Jim?"

"Yes, it's us."

"You guys look completely unrecognizable, and it's lucky that my parents just went out," she says, touching our faces. "Why are you guys here, anyway?"

"We left in a hurry and wanted to know what occurred after we departed also we wanted to make sure you are okay. Can you fill us in on the details?"

"They took me to the kitchen and integrated me, subjecting me to surveillance."

She strolls over to the window and slightly opens a section of blinds, motioning us to come over. "There is only one cruiser now. There used to be two; I guess they are getting bored."

"What about you guys? You look good."

"There are quite a lot of things to say."

"I apologize for forgetting my manners. Can I get you something to drink or eat?" Connie inquires, her eyes still taking in our new appearances.

"I'm good," I reply.

"Jim, do you want something?"

He shakes his head. "Thank you; I'm good."

"Please sit down," Connie tells us, pointing to the couch.

Connie joins us, sitting in a chair with her arms crossed, gazing at us.

"How is Dawna?"

I explained the events that occurred, "Everything is good now," I respond.

Standing up, she says, "Okay," with determination in her voice. "Where are you guys heading off to now?" Connie asks, her eyes darting from side to side, searching for an answer.

"We were going to do some grocery shopping."

"I'll join you. I need to grab a few things! Wait here. Let me grab my wallet."

With a sense of urgency, Connie dashes down the hallway, her green suede pants making a soft metallic noise.

"Okay, we can go," she says.

Jim and I turn our heads briefly toward one another.

"What?" she asks, her eyebrows furrowing in confusion. "Did you secretly wish to teleport there?" she taps her foot.

"That was the idea, in fact," I confirm.

"Well, that is a bad idea. It is still daylight, so you will be seen. Come, I'll drive," she says, walking toward the door.

After a brief exchange of glances between Jim and me and a shrug, we follow Connie outside. We finally reach her red sedan, and I find myself sitting next to her, with Jim comfortably positioned in the back. The engine starts, and we begin to reverse, and I grab the handle on top of the window.

Making our way up the road, we take a left turn and pass a lady gracefully walking with a cane. After driving for a few minutes, we reach the grocery store's parking lot. As we exit the car and begin strolling toward the store, we notice there doesn't seem to be anyone else around, however, the bright green glow of the neon sign assures us it is open for business.

With a graceful motion, the door slides open, as if it senses our presence and is welcoming us inside.

"I'll get the cart," Jim says, his footsteps fading as he walks away.

I glance in his direction, giving a slight nod, before my gaze shifts to Connie.

"Which aisle should we go in first?" I ask.

"I was thinking we could head to the produce section, since it's just ahead," she suggests, briefly pointing, just as Jim approaches with a shopping cart.

"Let's go," Jim says.

We pause while Connie selects different fruits and places them in the cart, and then we head over to the meat area. I quickly grab a few frozen chicken legs and toss them in.

"Nairb, your amulet is emitting a faint glow," Connie points out.

"This is really bad timing; it's just my luck," I tell her. "Jim!" I shout.

He quickly comes over, dropping a juice container in the cart.

"What do we do?" he asks, his voice uncertain.

"I will make a crack to the cottage, and you guys go," I instruct them, hearing screaming.

Connie exclaims anxiously, "But you will be noticed!"

The aisle is bathed in a radiant, bright light, emphasizing her resigned words, "I have no choice."

Glancing over my shoulder, I notice a dark, ominous shadow trailing behind me.

"Go go," Jim pushes the cart forward, and Connie's footsteps echo behind him.

As I turn my head, I hear the distinct gulp sound as they both step into the crack. As the shadow approaches me, its bloodshot eyes gleam with menace, and its sharp claws swipe through the air. Right before I step into the crack, a sharp needle prick jolts me, piercing just below my right shoulder. I feel a slow, deliberate hit against my ribs, causing a sharp pain to radiate throughout my body. Looking down, I see the jagged finger that tore my shirt, its force propelling me forward and bending my back. Pushed into the crack, Jim catches me, and the shadow charges in right behind. A loud and menacing growl fills the room, causing a chill to run down my spine, as if an invisible barrier is preventing the shadow from entering the crack.

We all gaze in horror as the black, angry shadow flies from left to right, its bloodshot eyes fixated on me. Its fingers are razor sharp and pointy.

The crack finally closes, and the shadow disappears, leaving me staring at the empty space, with a clenched jaw.

"Nairb, you have been hurt!" As she comes closer, Dawna pulls off the towel from her head.

"No worries, just a minor scratch."

"A scratch? You have blood all over; take off your shirt," she orders, gazing at me with wide eyes.

Removing my green shirt, I haphazardly throw it crumpled onto the couch and shift my focus downward.

Using water from her bottle, Dawna dampens the towel and proceeds to gently scrub my bloodstain, exposing a small puncture from the shadow.

"Look, you have a hole. It's closing," Dawna says, gazing at it.

The hole holds our attention as it steadily diminishes in size, revealing a vivid, bloody hue within but no signs of bleeding. It disappears entirely within a matter of seconds, leaving behind nothing but a bloodstain encircling the wound. With a delicate touch, Dawna removes the remaining blood from my shoulder and cleans the area around my wound.

Stepped back, satisfied, she says, "Nothing to be found, all clean."

"Thanks, Dawna."

She turns her head slightly and says, "No problem. Connie, I'm sorry about earlier."

"Nairb gave me a thorough explanation, Dawna, so there's no need to fret. Besides, I had an intuition that something was amiss."

"Thank you," Dawna replies, her voice tinged with remorse, as she walks up to Connie and wraps her arms around her.

"Well, that was interesting," Jim says, his eyes darting around, searching for more information.

Observing the full cart, Dawna remarks, "I see you've been busy with the grocery shopping."

"Yes, we grabbed a few things," Jim says, running his fingers over the items.

"Why didn't you wake me, Jim?"

"I didn't want to disturb you. You looked so peaceful."

"Well, how about we prepare something to eat, Dawna?" Connie asks.

"Yes, sounds like a plan."

"Jim, can you please push the shopping cart into the kitchen?" Connie inquires.

"Yes, I'm on it."

"Thanks."

"Well, I'm going to take a shower. I feel dirty. Are there any spare clothes here, Dawna?" I ask.

"Yes, in that white drawer in the washroom, but I think they are Patty's."

"I'm sure I'll find something."

While I leisurely stroll to the washroom, Jim leads the way to the kitchen, pushing the shopping cart, with Dawna and Connie trailing right behind him.

I turn on the water, and steam slowly forms on the shower glass, creating a hazy atmosphere. I enter and catch sight of my glowing scar once more. I casually poke it a few times, nonchalantly shrugging my shoulders, and then reach out to grab the soap from the white shower caddy, which holds an abundance of bottles.

After lathering and rinsing myself off, I reach for the towel on the right and rub my skin dry before opening the drawer on the left wall. Surrounded by a sea of pink, I couldn't contain my excitement as I mixed everything together, my face frozen in a silent scream.

As I adorned myself in shades of pink, I was pleasantly surprised to discover that every garment fit me flawlessly, as if it were custom-made.

"What's going on over here?" Everyone turned their head.

"Come on, they made some delicious food, and it is waiting for you," Jim says eagerly.

As I approach the kitchen table, the scent of the food wafts through the air, tempting me to sit down and indulge.

The clinking of utensils permeates the air as everyone fills their plates. Just as I am about to take a bite, a soft, eerie blue light illuminates the room, bringing everything to a halt. We exchange glances, surrounded by the faint sound of crickets chirping.

CHAPTER 15: FOOD

The cricket's rhythmic chirping is the only sound, and our eyes dart around in sync, taking in our surroundings.

"Don't worry," Jim says confidently. "This place is completely secure. Nothing can get inside here. I remember Patty said that," he says, lifting his fork piled with mashed potatoes.

"Let's hope she's right," I respond, my gaze shifting as I resume my meal.

As we eat, we reminisce about our past funny situations, which brings smiles to all of our faces. My head swivels from left to right, taking in the scene as we momentarily escape from our troubles and revel in each other's presence.

"Nairb, do you remember that peaceful beach we visited near the cliff?" Jim ask.

"With those massive gray rocks?"

"Do you think we can go there now after we finish eating?"

"Yes, we can, but as soon as my amulet goes blue, we are out of there."

"Get ready, everyone! We're going swimming," Jim announces.

The table empties, the girls excitedly making their way to the bedroom to get some clothes to swim in.

"Jim, you're not going?"

"Nah, no need. My boxers will do. What about you?"

"Same, but I don't have boxers but pink ladies' underwear."

"We'll have to make a stop for shopping and get you some clothes."

Dawna and Connie walked out.

Dawna said, "Okay, we're ready."

"Nairb, do the honors," Jim instructs, his finger indicating the empty space by the TV, as a sense of importance resonates in his voice.

The room is suddenly filled with a bright, illuminating light that emits a soft buzzing sound; an image of crystal blue water and sparkly yellow sand appears inside. Dawna and Connie approach, their bare feet sinking into the soft sand, the pink sandals next to them, and the pink towels draped over their shoulders.

With a quick glance in my direction, Jim heads toward the crack and disappears into it. I follow his lead, feeling the warmth of the yellow sand beneath my feet.

With excitement in their eyes, Dawna and Connie abandon their towels and race into the water, the sound of their laughter echoing along the sandy beach. Quickly, I turn my head and raise my hand to my eyebrows, trying to get a better view of my friends as they splash around.

"Ready, Nairb?" Jim says with a mischievous grin as he slips off his socks.

"Yes, just say when," I reply, bracing myself for action.

With a burst of energy, Jim dashes and shouts, "Go!"

I run after him, my pink bathrobe slipping off and landing on the soft sand while I shouted, "Hey!"

As Jim leaps into the water, his arms stretch out in front of him, creating a small splash that dances in the air. I follow closely, just a few seconds behind, trying to catch up.

Water sprays in every direction as Jim submerges himself, causing streams of water to drip onto my face and taste salty.

With only our heads above water, we close our eyes and embrace the gentle lift and drop of the waves, momentarily forgetting our worries. I take a deep breath, inhaling the smell of the salty sea air and listening to the sound of the water crashing against the sandy beach. We savor the moment, our eyes widening as we behold the shimmering rays dancing on the water's surface, compelling us to stand motionless in the liquid embrace that feels like a cozy, downy blanket we are reluctant to part with.

Squinting, Jim says, "We should get out."

Our heads instinctively turn as the water gradually reaches our stomachs, and we feel the soft sand beneath our feet shifting with each movement of the water.

"Nairb, thanks for taking us here," Connie says, expressing her gratitude.

"Yes, thank you," Dawna says.

The sand is warm beneath my feet as I say, "Don't worry about it. I wanted to."

As Connie picks up her towel, Jim runs up beside me and slaps me on the shoulder. "This is great," he comments, a smile spreading across his face.

"Indeed, it is."

"Nairb, your face looks flushed," Connie exclaims, massaging her head upside down.

"Thank you for noticing," I said with a genuine smile.

"You're welcome," she said graciously, her voice filled with sincerity.

"Hey, Dawna, can I borrow your towel once you finish using it?" Jim asked.

"Yep, all done," she said with a smile. Here you go," she said, handing Jim the soft, fluffy towel.

"There's a place I think you guys might find appealing," I tell them.

"Please share," Connie says.

"Where is it?" Jim inquires, his eyes gleaming with anticipation.

"You will have to see," I reply, as Dawna and Connie approach the crack.

Jim gazes at me briefly, then steps in.

When I join them, I immediately hear Dawna say, "Nairb, guys, check out how beautiful this glow is."

"Yes," Jim and Connie say in perfect synchronization, their agreement evident in their unified response.

"I had no idea you were so captivated by picturesque landscapes," Jim says.

"There are only a few places I know that are like this."

The giant orange orb casts its shimmering reflection on the water, creating a mesmerizing spectacle. One could easily lose track of time gazing at it.

"This place has such beautiful scenery. I had intended to bring Grace here."

"I'm sure she's here," Jim says, his hand rubbing my back as we marvel. "Why don't you go places now? I'm sure she will follow you, like you said."

I nod, my weary eyes staring back at me in the reflection.

"Dawna, Connie, we are heading to a different place, where the warm breeze will embrace us," Jim shouts, facing them. Turnes his head towards me, "It is warm, right?"

As Jim turns and walks into the crack, I see the moving light reflecting off his shoulder. Walking by my side, Dawna and Connie cautiously survey the area ahead before stepping forward. As I stand there, I feel the orange light penetrating my eyes, forcing me to wait a few moments before I can adjust. Eventually, I make my way to the crack, take a brief glance back, then step in.

Dawna's voice echoes in the darkness as she exclaims, "There is nothing here! It's completely dark."

Jim moves his head around, taking in his surroundings, before finally nodding in agreement. "I'm sorry, buddy. She is right." Jim gazes at me.

"It's because you guys are looking in the wrong direction. Look up," I instruct. They tilt their heads simultaneously, creating a synchronized movement, and the light dances and shimmers in the reflection of everyone's eyes.

"Wow, Nairb," Dawna says, her voice filled with astonishment. "Look at all these lights," she exclaims, her eyes widening in awe.

Connie stands motionless as the light ceases to reflect against her, engulfing her in a quiet darkness.

Dawna lowers her head, her voice filled with curiosity. "How did you come to learn about this place?"

"When I was younger, my dad would bring me here to stargaze. Do you see that bright star over there?" I ask, pointing.

"Yes, I see it," she nods, her gaze fixed on the magnificent sight before her. Gazing up, she marvels at the vast expanse of the night sky.

"To the left is another bright star, and to the left, down from it, creates Aries."

"Are there any different signs too? What is that white thing flying high up?" Dawna inquires.

Connie and Jim's heads swivel in unison, their eyes widening at the sight before them.

"Look," exclaims Jim, "It's moving even faster!"

As we observe a bright, exploding flash of light upon our eyes, we hear a loud growl.

"Your amulet is glowing," Jim announces.

I look down at it. "We better go."

"Well?"

"It's not working."

"What do you mean it's not working?"

"It's not working. Run left, you guys, now!" I shout, hearing a closer growl.

"Nairb, I don't see anything," Connie says.

"Just run; there should be a small old church soon."

"A church?"

"Yes, a church."

Worriedly, she asks, "Will we be safe there?"

"We will soon find out."

"There is an orange light over there," Dawna says, nodding her head in that direction.

"Yes, run toward that," I reply.

"Wait, I left my slipper behind!" Dawna says, turning head to look behind her.

"Don't worry about it. I lost mine a few minutes ago."

Dawna's gaze falls to the ground, and her other slipper slips away from her in a moment of distraction. As we dash, there is a moment of silence, where all we can hear is the sound of our own gasping breaths.

Just as we veer slightly to the right, a thunderous roar erupts from behind, sending chills down my spine.

As I scream, my voice trembles with fear and desperation.

"What, what's wrong?" Jim asks, his voice filled with hesitation as he carefully pronounces each word.

"A sharp scrape sent a shiver of coldness and pain down my back, leaving me with a lingering ache."

Jim notices, "Your shirt is torn at the back, and you have a long gash."

"We have to split up," I shout urgently. "Run toward the light and enter the church."

"No, Nairb," Jim exclaims, shaking his head. "That is a terrible idea."

"Don't hesitate, just do it!" I urge; my words filled with determination. "It's after me. Turn now!"

The three of them start to run toward the light, and I dash forward, following a sinuous path into the darkness, my footsteps echoing in the silence, a shiver running down my back and chest.

After a few seemingly endless seconds, I finally turn my head and watch their silhouettes fade into the distance. With a smile, I reassure myself they will be alright, before turning my gaze forward and sprinting into the darkness.

I feel the looming presence right behind me, sending shivers down my spine. Reluctant to face the inevitable,

I grit my teeth and propel myself forward with every ounce of energy I can muster.

As the pain travels down my back, I tightly clench my fists, determined not to let out a single sound that might indicate the injury's impact. My fists tighten, a testament to my determination as I prepare for my final stand. As I plan my attack, a blur of motion catches my attention. Grace flies by my shoulder, her speed making it impossible to clearly see her, before she collides with a shadow and creates a dazzling burst of white light. As I squint and hear growls, a loud voice commands me to run. Without hesitation, I spin around and dash toward the flickering orange light. With a turn of my head, the once vibrant light diminishes, swallowed by the encroaching darkness. The sound of a menacing growl fills my ears, causing me to dash even faster and glance anxiously behind me. Gasping and feeling my muscles cramping, I strain to hear and see Jim, Dawna, and Connie motioning for me to come in, their urgent yells echoing through the air.

The roaring behind me grows louder, and I see the sharp black fingers on both sides, their ominous movement drawing closer. I instinctively leap forward, hands raised above my head.

CHAPTER 16: FORWARD

With the help of my friends holding the church door open, I leap inside, only to feel a chilling brush against my leg as a black finger grazes the air. The sensation sends me into a frenzy, screaming uncontrollably as I tumble onto the worn wooden floor.

The shadow swiftly ascends, narrowly avoiding the church's spires, while my amulet emits a faint, blue luminescence.

"Are you okay?" Dawna asks, her fingers hovering near her mouth.

"Yes," I reply, my scratchy voice barely audible.

Jim's hand tightens around mine as he exclaims, "That was close!"

"How did you know the church would work?" Connie inquires.

Standing up, I declare, "I didn't."

"Luckily, it worked out for the best." Jim responds.

The sound of squeaking wood boards accompanies my pacing, while my amulet continues to glow, casting an otherworldly light.

"What are we going to do?" Jim's eyes widen with worry.

"I don't know exactly, but it's nearby. I can tell because my amulet is still emitting a faint glow."

"Can we use the holy water that is there?" Connie points at it.

"Do you wish to determine if it actually works? How should we go about squirting it?" I say.

We all look at each other, realizing we will probably be stuck here for quite some time.

Moving his eyes around, Jim comments on the comforting warmth in the area.

"Well, for now, let's just sink into those worn brown benches and get comfortable," I say, walking over to one.

One by one, we stroll over and find a seat, our heads gently swaying along with the flickering orange light that casts a cozy, comforting glow, instantly putting us at ease.

"I'm sure someone will come here in the morning." I announce. "Let's just rest for now. Until my power returns."

Everyone lays on their side, propping their head on their arm, and peacefully close their eyes. Sliding down, my mind is consumed with thoughts of Grace as darkness descends upon me.

As the earthquake struck, the ground trembled violently beneath me, causing everything around to sway and topple.

In a panic, I sought refuge under the sturdy wooden kitchen table in the cottage.

"Wake up, Nairb. The crack appeared," Jim shouts, shaking me.

The moment I open my eyes, I catch sight of the crack and quickly sit up, my eyes swiftly turning toward the TV I see in it.

"Quickly, go wake up Dawna and Connie!" I exclaim with wide eyes.

In a rush, Jim darts toward the other row of benches, his voice piercing the air with screams. Dawna and Connie exclaim simultaneously, "What?"

"The crack, hurry!"

They shoot up from their seats, their heads turning as they stand and dash toward the flickering, buzzing light.

"Run everyone! I'll be right behind you," I exclaim, getting up.

I dash in behind them, and within seconds, the light begins to shrink behind us.

"Wow, that was a close one," Dawna exclaims, her hair disheveled.

"Yes, it was. What happened?" Connie asks, gazing at me.

"It's hard to explain, but in my dream, I was transported to this specific spot. As soon as I arrived, the earth began to quake violently, and there, amidst the chaos, stood Jim."

"I'm so happy you dreamed about this place!" she exclaims, her eyes shining joyfully. Connie walks up to me, placing a reassuring hand on my shoulder, and we stroll together to the kitchen.

"I'm curious about what happened." I scratch my head.

"Don't worry about it," Jim says, briefly touching my shoulder, then casually walking away.

"Ya, don't worry, Nairb." Opening the fridge door, Connie declares, "We are here, and that's all that counts."

"You are right, guys."

"Do you want any chips?" As Jim holds up a blue bag, it stands out against the background, demanding my attention.

"No, thank you. Maybe later."

"I don't think there will be a later."

My gaze shifts to him, as he places the blue bag of chips on the wooden table, the sound of his munching echoing around the room.

With a quick scan from left to right, I ask where Dawna is.

"I saw her going to the washroom," Jim answers, munching away.

"I think we should eat some breakfast."

Connie takes something out of the fridge and says, "I'm already one step ahead of you."

I nod in agreement, my stomach growling.

"Hey Nairb, check out the crack that just appeared."

"That's odd. I just had the clothing store in mind. Can you see if there are any clothing racks?"

Walking in front of the crack, Jim takes a moment to gaze inside, and he remarks, "Yes, it looks closed, too."

"Okay, do you want to go through it? I need to get changed."

"Let's do it!"

"You guys, I really don't think that's a good idea. "We just got back. What if you get stuck again?"

"Relax, Connie, this is close to Jim's house. Plus, we won't be long."

I approach Jim and ask, "Are you ready?"

Jim nods his head.

"Alright, here I go," I say, turning around and looking at the bright light, then stepping into the aisle filled with jeans, Jim right behind me.

"Great, Jim. Find your size." I instruct, looking around the room. "Hurry up; they have everything," I say, grabbing a pair of black denim.

Jim dashes around, collecting shirts from different aisles.

"We don't have time for you to browse; just get whatever," I tell him, piling clothes on my right arm.

"Almost done," Jim exclaims, quickly snatching a pair of socks and placing it on top of the other items he has in his arms. "There," he says, dashing next to me.

I turn and glance at the aisle, taking in the emptiness and the smooth, black carpet beneath my feet.

The aisle is brightened by a light as Dawna appears, holding a plate.

I turn my head, feeling a rush of anticipation. "Ready?"

Jim moves his head up and down.

"Let's go," I say.

As the light moves across the black jeans, the aisle becomes a captivating display of illumination. We start to move forward, and the light fades away, causing everything around us to plunge into darkness.

I furrow my brow, puzzled, as I glance back at the empty spot. "That's curious," I comment.

"Just try again," Jim says.

"Nothing is happening."

"Nairb, your amulet has turned blue and is glowing."

I avert my gaze downwards, spin around, and repeat, "Jim, drop your clothes now! We need to find somewhere to hide!"

"Hurry, Jim, follow me," I motion with a quick wave of my hand. Hurriedly, we dash to the changing room, the sound of our breathing filling the air.

Placing my finger against my lips, I softly whisper, "It's here," as I peek at the edge of the black drape.

The shadow glides through the aisle where Jim and I were, its black flames fully engulfed. Moving the coat rack with thick blue jackets hanging, it sniffs our dropped clothes and lets out a soft squeak. With a slow movement, it raises its head, and its bloodshot eyes survey the area, before it turns its head left to right and lowers it back down. With its pointy black fingers extending cautiously, it moves forward at a slow pace. I hear the sound of its breath as it releases the air it has taken in. As I stand in front of the change room, I notice Jim's hands resting on his stomach.

"Is it gone?" Jim murmurs in a low voice.

"Shhh, don't make any noise."

With a tap of his foot on the ground, Jim catches the attention of the shadow, causing it to abruptly shift its gaze toward us. After a momentary pause, it begins to approach us. Stepping back, I instinctively place my finger by my mouth and lock eyes with Jim. The curtains inch forward, causing our eyes to widen in disbelief as we stand frozen in place.

The yellow rings on the top left of the curtain slowly glide to the right, creating a gentle clicking sound as they touch one another, then abruptly come to a stop. The curtain gently lifts and lowers, filling the room with the sound of a loud, explosive rush of air, before settling back down. A loud thud echoes through the room as if a heavy box has crashed to the ground, causing the curtains to sway back and forth.

"What are you doing?" Pale and barely audible, Jim whispers softly.

Slowly grabbing the end of the curtains, I cautiously turn my head to look outside, whispering, "I'm going to take a peek. Stay quiet."

I briefly turn my head forward and continue to scan the area slowly.

"Well, what do you see?" Jim asks, starting to walk over to me.

"I don't see it; I think it's gone," I say.

Carefully sliding the curtains open, I cautiously peek outside, taking a moment to scan in both directions before proceeding.

Sliding the curtain to the right, I motion with my hand, then whisper, "All clear, let's go."

With each slow and deliberate step, I glance in both directions, making sure to check for any signs of danger, as Jim faithfully follows in my footsteps.

"Quickly, grab our stuff," I instruct, rushing through the aisle, with the sound of our footsteps echoing.

After we pick our clothes back up, Jim whispers, "Now what?"

"Follow me," I say, quickly but quietly jogging toward the exit glass doors.

Opening one slowly, I cautiously poke my head out, swiveling it left and right.

"Okay, let's go," I say, and we run down the empty semi-dark halfway, hearing a soft echo with each step.

I open the light green glass door, and as we step inside a fancy clothing store, I notice Jim glancing around twice.

I whisper, "To the back," and we carefully make our way through the dimly lit room.

Jogging through the aisle, I feel the rough texture of jackets brushing against me.

The sound of a low, guttural growl fills the air, causing us to freeze in place.

"Hurry up, we need to leave now," I said, grabbing a shoe.

"Now where?" Jim asks, his voice filled with confusion.

The growl reverberates through the air, sounding dangerously close.

"Over there, you'll find an exit that leads to the roof," I say, pointing in the direction.

"The roof?"

"Yes, the roof," I tell him, starting to dash that way.

"How do you know this?"

"I used to work here."

Reaching the blue steel door labeled "Emergency Exit," Jim comments, "I didn't know you worked here."

A menacing growl and the sound of glass shattering fills the air, urging me to quickly swing the door open and make a frantic dash through it.

Hearing the loud roar as the door closes, I turn my head and am met with the sight of the dark flames and the bloody eyes locking onto me, growling as it swiftly charges in our direction.

"Run faster, Jim!"

Jim turns his head, his eyes widening as he mutters, "Oh crap." As he dashes beside me, I hear the crunchy sound of his steps on the black, shiny surface.

"Nairb, the roof is reaching its end."

"I see that," I say, coming to a halt a few seconds later near the roof's edge.

"Jump, Jim," I order, looking down.

"Are you crazy? It's like ten meters down."

My gaze is fixed downward when, out of nowhere, a crack forms above the yellow car; Dawna and Connie are sitting in the kitchen by the table at the bottom of the crack.

"Jump!" I shout, the sound of my voice echoing through the air.

In a split second, I give Jim a forceful shove, propelling him downward.

CHAPTER 17: FALL

Jim starts to scream, but without hesitation, I look down and jump right after him. As I turn my back, I face a looming shadow, its growls amplified by the intensifying black flames.

I gracefully soar through the crack, descending beside Jim, with a resounding thump on the hardwood floor that casts ethereal blue beams of light. I avert my gaze to find Jim swaying back and forth, but the shadow's eyes meet mine, and I can't look away from its bloodshot eyes, leaking a red substance that lingers for a few moments before the crack disappears, with the soothing blue glow reflecting off the hardwood floor.

Dawna and Connie rush over to us, swiftly dropping down to a squatting position.

"What happened?" Connie asks, her voice filled with concern.

"We had a hiccup."

As I stand up, Jim turns his head toward me.

"Yes, a hiccup."

"A hiccup?" Connie asks in confusion.

"The details don't matter, but hey, we did get some clothes," I say, holding up the black jeans.

"I'm glad you're back. The new clothes will look better. Come to the kitchen; We made a snack," Connie says, patting my chest and getting up.

A multilayered sandwich catches my eye as I sit at the table.

"Is this a fried egg?" I ask, lifting the sandwich, and feeling the warm, gooey yellow stuff ooze onto my fingers.

"Yes, it is," she replies, with a nod and a smile. I indulge in the satisfying crunchiness.

With my mouth full, I exclaim, "This is amazing!"

"I'm glad you like it; how about you, Jim?"

"It's so good; I'm going for another satisfying crunch."

"Why aren't any of you eating?" While holding the sandwich, I inquired.

"Dawna and I had already eaten; since your return was delayed, we decided to eat, sorry."

With a relaxed stride, she approached Dawna, downplaying the significance of the comment with a dismissive wave and a casual "No big deal."

"I see you got your clothes," Dawna says, holding up a shirt and examining it.

"Jim couldn't find his size, so he got this one," Jim briefly looks at me. "I think I figured it out, Jim."

"Figured what out?"

"When I try to make a crack appear too much or when I'm tired, it doesn't work, and the same applies to my healing. I can use it a few times before requiring regeneration.”

“It does make sense, quite interesting indeed.”

“So, does that mean we can go to my house later?” Dawna asks, her voice filled with anticipation.

“Why exactly?” I question, gazing at her.

“To pick up some bank notes.”

“We have bank notes?” Jim inquires, moving his head.

“Yes, under the plate in the kitchen cupboard. What do you say, Nairb, unless we can visit your local bank?”

“Sure, we can go, but it’ll have to be in a few hours, alright?”

“Once you all finish eating, we can settle down and watch a movie.”

“I would like to change first,” I say.

“Yes, me too,” Jim agrees, gazing at Dawna.

“That’s fine, you guys.”

As we finish our meal, Jim and I rise from our seats and begin a relaxed stroll toward our disheveled piles of clothing. I take the lead, heading to the washroom, while Jim follows closely behind, heading to the bedroom.

After we have changed, we head to the living room to watch a movie. I drop down next to Jim, and we choose a comedy film from the collection of old VHS tapes, popping it in the black VCR player. As the hours pass, my mind finds a rare sense of tranquility, almost forgetting about my powers.

Grace leaves to use the washroom, leaving me in an eerie darkness.

On the TV screen, vibrant colors and sharp white lines catch my attention, and I glance around and realize I'm alone on the couch.

"Hey, what happened?" I turn and ask Jim, who is standing by the kitchen sink, filling a glass with water.

"Nothing happened. You started to snore, and we left quietly."

"Was I sleeping long?"

"Just a few hours."

"Where are the girls?"

"They are outside, checking things out."

Dawna walks in, "Look who's awake. You had a nice nap?"

"Yes, sorry I missed the movie."

"Don't worry about it. We ended it early. It was just too exciting."

Connie walks in, "Welcome back."

"Dawna was just saying how exciting the movie was."

"Yes, we had to shut it off early. It just was too good."

"So Nairb, do you think we can go to Jim's and my house?"

"Yes, I don't see why not. I'm fully refreshed." I gaze at Jim briefly.

"Just to our garage, in case someone sees the light; I'm sure someone is watching it."

"Yes, good idea, Jim," Dawna says.

The room is filled with an ethereal white light that seems to be in constant motion, casting shimmering rays that resemble sparkling water, causing everyone to squint.

"Shall we go?" I say.

"After you, Dawna," Jim motions with his hand.

"Thank you," Dawna strolls into the crack, with Jim right behind her.

"You're not going, Connie?"

"No, someone has to clean up."

I swirl my head from left to right. "It looks clean to me."

"What exactly are those yellow objects on the ground?" Pointing.

"Oh, ah, don't worry about it now."

"It's okay, go. I'll be fine."

"Are you sure?"

"Yes, now go!"

"Okay, we won't be long," I tell her, turning and walking through the crack.

I meet Jim and Dawna on the other side.

"Everything okay? I saw you talking to Connie."

"Yes, everything is fine. Connie is staying behind."

"Okay, let's go."

Dawna guides the way, the garage illuminated by the light dancing on the walls, accompanied by a subtle scent of burned oil near the sleek red sports car, with tinted windows that conceal the view from outside.

"When did you get this?" I ask, pointing to the red shiny hood.

"Last week, I believe."

"And you didn't tell me."

"It's not ready yet, plus now I don't have to tell you."

Dawna opens the brown wooden door, and Jim and I enter, and I notice the faint scent of bread.

Dawna follows, and the room plunges into darkness as the lights go off.

She walks to the kitchen, saying she'll be right back.

Jim and I approach a window in the front, its view obstructed by sturdy brown boards.

He lightly lifts a board toward him and takes a peek. "I knew it. There is a white car parked out there."

"Let me see," I say, as Jim takes a step back.

I gently lower the board, and as I turn to Jim, I see the living room walls become awash with blue rays, illuminating the entire room shortly after.

"Nairb, your amulet."

I quickly glance and shout, "Dawna, we must leave immediately."

She runs toward us.

"Let's go, quickly. No time to ask questions."

With a burst of energy, Jim follows closely behind Dawna as I begin to slowly walk backwards, moving my head from left to right. As I enter the crack, I witness the window shattering, with shards of glass soaring through the room. I swiftly move my head, narrowly avoiding one of the sharp pieces, but the other fragment grazes my cheek. My eyes are fixed on the scene before me as the boards tremble and gave way, revealing a haunting sight—long, slender fingers creeping out.

The view of the room disappears, and the bright light with the blue illumination with it, and I turn around.

Connie rushes toward me, holding a napkin, and says, "Nairb, your cheek is bleeding," before stopping in front of me.

"Don't worry, Connie," I say, as I feel my cheek begin to heal.

"Oops, I forgot you could do that, but you still have a red mark. Let me take care of it." She licks the napkin and rubs my cheek. As our eyes briefly meet, she smiles and walks away.

"I'm going to see Grace," I announce. All eyes are suddenly on me. "I wanted to go earlier."

"Nairb, let me go with you."

"Sorry, Jim. I need to do this alone. Besides, I'm safe at the graveyard," The room starts to light up.

Stepping onto the gray gravel rocks, I swiftly dash past the black open gate, which is gently illuminated by a soft yellow light from the green light post. The bright moonlight directs my path, while a dark blanket covers my side vision. I pass a few gray stones with dark brown wooden crosses.

With a burst of energy, I charge forward, my voice echoing through the air as I shout Grace's name. I abruptly halt in front of a somber black tombstone adorned with a single Hugo Victor rose. A small, sturdy candle stands beside it, its flame swaying gently from side to side, casting a warm, golden light on the flower.

"Grace," I yell, turning in all directions. "Grace!" I shout again.

"I'm here, Nairb," she calls, and I see her standing on top of a tombstone.

"Grace, are you all right? You blew up." I notice a brown wooden cross behind her brightened by a yellow moving light.

"Yes, I'm fine. I can only slow it down if I leave," she replies.

"That is a relief. It shows everywhere I go. How?"

"It has the same ability as you and can change shapes, hypnotize people, or enter them."

"This explains a lot."

"Nairb, thank you for showing me those places. They were beautiful."

"I'm glad you liked them. It was not easy showing them to you without you really being there physically."

"I'm glad you did. It made me smile and know how lucky I was to have met you."

"Grace, can't you just return?" I inquire, sniffling, and with blurry vision.

"I wish it was that easy. There are some things I can't do. We all have a purpose, even if we don't understand it."

"And what is your purpose?"

"To help you understand."

"Understand what? That you left."

"There are important things happening that I wish to share with you, but you're not ready to hear them yet."

"Grace, I don't want any of this! It can all be taken back, and we can go home," I say, streaks going down my cheeks.

With glossy eyes, she says, "I wish it was that simple."

"Simply go ahead and do it."

"I really wish I could. I need you to be strong. Now pull yourself up, mister. You have something to do."

I rub my nose against my arm, then nod.

The black tombstone seems to come alive as the moving lights cast shimmering reflections upon it.

"Be ready," I say, turning and strolling in.

"I know what I have to do!" I say, seeing my friends. All heads turn in unison.

"What do you mean, Nairb?" Connie questions, a bright white spot of light dancing around on her clothes.

"I'm going to lead the shadow to Grace. I thought about this before, and it's time to end it."

"I'm coming with you, Nairb," Jim says, taking a step forward.

"Jim, you don't have to."

"Nonsense, you will need help." He stops in front of me.

The room grows darker, casting shadows across their faces. "Are you sure about this?" I ask.

"Yes, I'm sure. We can't hide forever with that thing; it's always around where I go.

Dawna glances at Jim, her silence speaking volumes about her concern. She then turns to me, her eyes widening as she places a finger in her mouth.

"What's the plan?" Jim asks.

"We are going to need a car," I say, the room brightening.

Jim as we stroll through the opening together.

"Hey, I know this dealership," Jim says, moving his head around.

"Well, you should. It's close to my parents. Let's go," I say, tapping his arm.

"Jim, choose a car." The vehicles, which were once shiny and immaculate, now look worn and weathered, with faded paint and rust spots.

"Wait, how are we going to take it, with no keys?"

"I'll show you. Just pick one."

"Okay, that black pickup truck," Jim says, pointing to it.

We run over to it.

"Okay, now what?" he asks, gazing at me.

"Watch." I squat down and run behind the truck, pulling out a key from the tailpipe.

"Well, I'll be, and this is the same for all the vehicles here?"

"Yes," I reply, opening the door.

"How do you know this?"

"Once, as a kid, I was hiding, and I saw the owner placing the key inside the tailpipe of each car. I'm surprised he still does it."

"You weren't sure?"

"No, it was still happening a few years ago, though."

"What if there was no key?"

"I would try Plan B."

"Plan B?"

"Yes, break a window and hot-wire the car," I say, smiling, turning the key lock.

Jim widens his eyes and becomes silent.

The truck gently vibrates, creating a soft hum that fills the air. A faint, white mist hovers around it, vanishing into nothingness as it rises from the back.

"Nairb, your amulet is glowing blue!" I look down. "Look, something black is headed this way, and something smaller is emerging from it, moving even faster. Watch out!" Jim pushes me.

CHAPTER 18: IT'S TIME

I instinctively duck as a sharp, black object comes hurtling toward me, narrowly missing my head, and embedding itself in the steel beside the driver's door.

"Jump in quickly," Jim says, hurriedly moving around the truck. "Quick, step on it! It's right behind us."

Glancing in the rearview mirror, I catch sight of the menacing black claws reaching toward me. As I focus on the road ahead, billows of white smoke engulfs our peripheral vision, accompanied by a loud screeching noise, forcing us deeper into our seats. As we drive away from the dealer's lot, the black leather seat jolts us with each bounce, accompanied by the melodic sounds of classical music filling the airwaves.

As I turn right onto the gray road, it emits a high-pitched squeak, and a gust of warm wind hits my face.

"Where is it?" Jim asks, turning his head in all directions.

"On your left, you'll find it right behind us."

I quickly glance in the rearview mirror and catch a glimpse of it before being jolted back by the thunderous roar of the engine. "Oh crap," I exclaim, feeling a rush of panic.

"What? What's happening?"

"We just flew by a cop car stationed on the side of the road." Jim turns his head to look at it.

"I see white, faint smoke behind the car."

With a quick glance in the rearview mirror, I respond, "Yes, I see him." The cruiser pulls onto the road and starts to follow us, its red lights flashing, the sound of sirens filling the air.

"What are we going to do?" Jim asks, his voice filled with worry.

"Pull over and show my license and registration." Jim turns his head to face me.

"Seriously?"

"No, of course not." My eyes reflect the red glow.

"Great, he wants you to pull over."

With each passing second, the cop car gets closer to us.

"I don't think he knows that black thing is following us, and that's why we're speeding."

Glancing in the rearview mirror, "I don't see anyone now, do you?"

Jim moves his head around. "Still there. How much longer do you think to the cemetery?"

"Maybe ten minutes."

"Watch out."

"I see him now he was in my blind-spot," as the engine starts to roar.

"We were nearly hit by that cop car! We have someone following us closely." Jim strains his eyes.

"Watch this," I say, and a loud bang occurs, right after being jerked forward from the seat's backrest driving over the curb. As I gaze at the rearview mirror, the gently moving scenery outside creates a soothing backdrop, accompanied by the faint sound of scraping. I clench my teeth, holding my tongue in anticipation.

"I can't believe you did that, Nairb."

"What are they going to do, arrest me?"

The loud banging on the roof sounds like heavy metallic raindrops threatening to pierce through. I briefly tilt my head upwards and then return my gaze ahead.

"What was that, Jim?"

"I don't know."

Just a few seconds later, a mysterious black object slices through the windshield, embedding itself firmly in the dashboard.

"What the heck!" Jim shouts, forcefully yanking it out.

"Hold on," I shout as the force pushes my body to the left, accompanied by a long, piercing squeak.

"Did you see that radiant burst of light, Nairb?" Jim asks, squinting.

"Yes, I saw. It must have been Grace."

"Grace? You think?"

"I can't really explain it now," I say, glancing at Jim quickly.

"Okay," Jim exclaims, turning his head back, with widened eyes. "That cop is gaining on us, on our right again."

As I turn my steering wheel to the right, I hear a crash, followed by scraping noises that occur intermittently as I attempt to turn left and move forward.

"Construction is taking place ahead!" Jim's hands slam against the dashboard as he screams.

The engine resounds with a deafening roar as the police cruiser roars alongside in unison. A loud screech fills the air as I slide forward, and in that moment, the cruiser speeds past me, the officer's hands in front of his face, before he collides with a cement truck.

I remain motionless, unable to move a muscle. Finally, I turn my head and body to look behind me. The cruiser comes zooming toward me, its sirens blaring, while the other cars on the road come to an eerie silence. I can feel the weight of everyone's gaze on me from their cars.

"What are we going to do?" Jim asks, his voice filled with panic and desperation.

The moment I shift the gear into reverse, the tires let out an ear-splitting screech, the sound echoing through the air. We race past the gray parking meter, leaving a trail of white smoke in our wake.

With a puzzled look, he questions, "What are you doing?"

The roaring engine drowns out all other sounds, and I spot the approaching cruiser just a few meters ahead. Squinting my eyes against the bright red lights, I quickly turn the steering wheel to the right, narrowly avoiding tipping the truck.

As the cruiser whizzes by me, I feel the rush of wind and catch a whiff of burning rubber from its tires.

I rev the engine, but Jim remains silent, focusing on what lies ahead.

"Jim," I say confidently, "I know a shortcut we can take."

With a slow and deliberate movement, his head turns, nodding in approval, before settling back into its original position. The road shimmers with a captivating red glow of light.

"I'm going to turn left," I tell Jim as we approach the street.

As I do, I'm startled by a roar coming from above. I glance up and press my foot down until I reach the maximum pressure.

"Jim, the cemetery is just up ahead."

The vehicle's backside skids across the uneven road, causing a large cloud of dirty brownish dust to billow out behind us. The truck slides, and the grinding of small rocks beneath us echoes through the air, causing the scenery to stop abruptly.

With a glance at Jim, I yell, "Run! Follow me!"

With a burst of energy, we swing the doors open and bolt toward the open gate, the ominous clouds rolling in and the sound of a halt echoing in our ears. The deafening roar from above grows even louder, causing me to quickly avert my gaze as Jim and I dash forward.

"To Grace's grave, Jim!" I exclaim, swiftly passing a black cross and leaping over a gray ceramic tombstone.

As we stop at the brown cross, a single Hugo Victor rose lays in the center of the black marble plate. A flickering candle reflects the shifting light as we turn around.

"Nairb, what should we do?" Jim asks, his voice filled with worry.

"I don't know," I say, my eyes fixated on the approaching group of people wearing various shades of black hats.

A roar echoes through the air, accompanied by the subtle glow of yellow candlelight reflecting off ceramic plates.

"I'm scared, Nairb."

"Don't be. Grace will save us."

The screams to raise our hands multiply, filling the air with a deafening sound that seems to originate just a few meters in front of us. As we lift them, we are surrounded by several individuals wearing blue-collared shirts. A sense of unease fills the air as they point a black object at us. Jim and I briefly lock eyes, then look forward, startled by a deafening roar. We instinctively look up, only to see everyone around us falling to the ground, like leaves from a tree branch. In front of me, I see a terrifying sight. A pair of black, bloodshot eyes glaring at me, accompanied by long, menacing fingers.

"Jim, when I say now, you jump to your right side."

"Okay," he responds faintly.

The shadow flies toward me, its roar piercing my ears, "Get ready, Jim. Okay, now!"

Leaping away, I quickly glance and witness the impact as it collides with the brown cross. The sight of hands made of white light causes my eyes to squint as they reach out and seize the growling shadow, yanking it down into the grave. Standing up, I am greeted by Jim running up beside me, and our hands clasp together in a friendly gesture. As we both gaze and squint, the growling shadow is pulled down, scraping the cross with its hands, and the light abruptly turns off, leaving us in a blanket of silence.

"It's over," I utter, gently returning the Hugo Victor rose and candle to their original places.

Taking a step back, my eyes struggle to focus on the black ceramic tile, causing everything to blur.

"Come," I say softly, tapping Jim's shoulder as I turn around.

A figure bathed in a bright, ethereal light appears, calling out, "Nairb!"

I look back and call out Grace!

"Yes, it's me, my dear."

"Hello, Grace, I was never really sure it was you until now," Jim says.

"Hi, Jim."

"Thank you for doing this, you guys."

"Nairb, you look like you again," Jim says.

"You too, Jim," I exclaim, touching his face.

"Dawna has been restored as well. When these officers wake up, they will not remember anything that has happened. Everything that was against you both is gone, like it never happened." Gazing at me, she says, "I cannot restore that what you wish for, though."

"Will I see you again?"

Putting her hand over my heart, she says, "As long as I'm here. I'll be always with you." Her glossy eyes reflect mine as she taps my chest.

"There must be another way?"

"I'm sorry, there isn't. You guys are free, and so am I. This has to be done. We will see each other again," she says, hovering a few steps back.

She looks at me, and a blanket of darkness and silence appear.

"Grace!" I call out, turning my head in multiple directions. "Grace!"

"I think she's gone, Nairb," Jim says softly.

"No, Jim. Grace!" I insist, my voice tinged with desperation.

Jim walks toward me, putting his hand on my shoulder. "She's gone, Nairb," he says gently.

I look around, a sense of defeat washing over me.

"Let's go back," I say, dejected.

I gaze at Jim, squinting with my blurry eyes, and within seconds, I catch sight of a brown cross reflecting nearby. Jim walks ahead, and I follow closely behind, pausing momentarily, before taking a step. I turn around and am greeted by the soothing sight of gentle, swaying orange light. Inhaling deeply, I take a step forward.

Jim and I glance at each other as the room illuminates a blue glow.

Bonus

As a bonus, please email a screenshot of your receipt to *gregsiofer@aboutnairb.com*. A website link to the images that were considered for the interior pages will be emailed to you.

Request

If you liked the story I've presented, please leave an honest review. Spread the word about this book. I want this story to reach as many people as possible.

Thank you,

Greg Siofer

http://www.aboutnairb.com

gregsiofer@aboutnairb.com

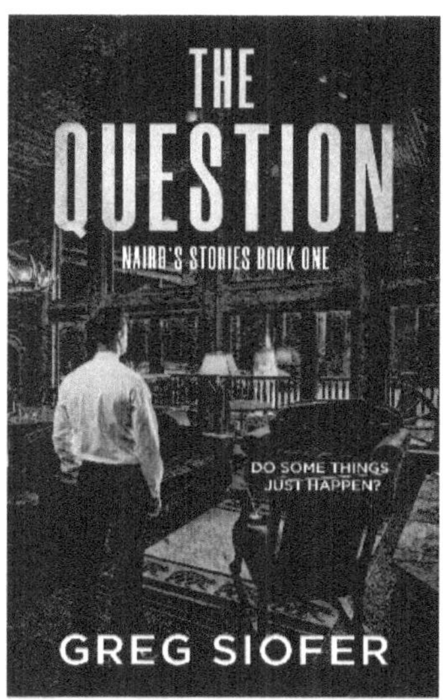

INTRUDER

Raising my head, I said, "You're right. Stay here, and I'll investigate."

Walking up the driveway, I quietly open the door on the left side of the house and step into the kitchen, leaving the door open wide. Keeping to the right wall, I slowly peek around. Suddenly I feel pressure on my left shoulder, as if someone wants my attention. I turned my head and saw Grace.

"What are you doing here? You are supposed to stay put!"

"I wanted to see," she whispers.

"See that knife on the counter?" I whisper back.

"Yes."

"Please get it for me, but do it quietly."

"Here it is." Grace hands me the kitchen knife.

Slowly, we slither along sideways, sticking to the wall. I hear something coming from upstairs. I turn to Grace and, with my index finger to my lips, I shush her and make gradual movements.

"Hear that?" I point to the location of the sound. "Quietly now."

We move casually, more to the side this time.

Grace sneezes, breaking the silence. "Crap," she mutters.

"Who's there?" Grace asks.

I glance at her. "Are you serious?"

A person bolts down the stairs, pointing a black gun in our direction and holding something shiny in their other hand, yelling for us to put our hands up. With our arms raised, I draw my eyes to the gold cross necklace sticking out of their left hand, which instantly turns red, forcing the intruder to drop everything and flee out the nearest door.

I look at Grace. "Are you alright that was scary? Do you mind picking up the gun and placing it on the table next to you? I'm going to call the police." I lower my hands.

Taking a few steps forward, I hear a bang and my body pushes forward. I twist around and see Grace standing with the gun in her hand.

"Why does my shirt feel wet on the right shoulder? Did you shoot just me with the gun?" I ask in disbelief, looking at the bloodstain.

"Oh my God! I'm so sorry Nairb, it was an accident. Stay still, and I'll be right back," Grace raises her hand towards my chest as she puts the gun on the table with the other, then rushes upstairs.

The cupboards in the washroom bang loudly. A minute later, Grace races down the stairs and stops in front of me.

As I take off my shirt, I said, "I thought getting shot might be a bit more painful." I clench my teeth and widen my eyes.

I point at the bullet wound with my index finger, and Grace inspects it.

"Look, Nairb, the hole is closing, and the bullet just popped out and fell to the ground."

Grace grabs a cloth from the table next to her and licks its end. She cleans the bloodstains from my shoulder.

"How come your hand has a cut on it?" I inquired when she was finished.

"As I passed you the kitchen knife, I cut myself."

"Let me see it." I take her right hand and open it.

The wound on her palm slowly heals.

"Look, the cut is disappearing," I exclaim.

"Grab the knife from the table."

Grace does as I request, pointing to my right forearm.

"Cut me!" I told her.

"Are you certain?"

"Yes."

Grace holds the knife near my right forearm.

"Are you sure?" She looks into my eyes.

"Yes. Grace, just do it." With that, she cuts.

Chapter 1

The Beginning of My Journey

Passing cars and seeing stars out the window, the cool night air blew in through the open windows as I hurried home. My wife (at the time) and I had some friends that were getting married soon, and we had invited them over for supper. I had not even had time to get the tortilla chips for the recipe we were planning to make. Hopefully, our friends would arrive late; maybe the traffic out of Toronto would slow them down.

I parked at the house and dashed straight into the kitchen. As I put the chicken and potatoes into the oven, my wife asked about the tortilla chips for the snack. Pretending I had not heard the question, I showed her the red wine I'd grabbed on the way home.

Just then, the doorbell rang. "They're here," I said to her. The table was set with plates, utensils, and wine glasses, and everything seemed ready for us to sit down. Our friends, Lizbeth and Tucker, came in and we all approached the table.

As our friends sat down, my wife went to the kitchen to put the final touches on the food, and I poured the wine to keep them occupied. I took a seat and said cheers and we began to drink from our glasses. Although it was only around 200 mL, and not a strong wine, I noticed that I was already starting to slur my words and get very fidgety as if I had been consuming hard liquor. Confused but not wanting to cause a scene, I pointedly ignored this strange behavior.

When we'd finished our wine, I apologized that we were missing the tortilla chips and offered to walk ten minutes to the convenience store to pick some up, but we decided to go after supper.

My wife and I left the table and went to the kitchen to check on the chicken and potatoes. The chicken was looking brown and juicy so we took it out of the oven and placed it on the counter, and the potatoes were perfectly crispy. We served Tucker and Lizbeth, and I was happy to see how well we had done even though I had been rushing to get things done in time.

With supper over, we walked down the road to the convenience store, glancing up at the stars and just talking about our future. We looked at the other nice houses in our neighborhood, seeing how people lived.

On the way back, I was a bit shaky and flimsy. Again, it felt like I had been drinking quite heavily earlier, which was not the case. I wondered what the heck was happening, but again I stayed silent and ignored whatever was going on, proceeding toward our house and admiring the multi-colored leaves of the trees along our gently curving path. Looking at the sky full of stars, the moon shining bright, and no clouds in sight, helped keep my mind off my body's sudden strangeness.

Back at the house, everything was lit up as if someone was home. We enjoyed a few of the beers that I always kept in the fridge in case of company, then made the snack with the tortilla chips, which turned out to be brownish and crunchy. We had a super time just mumbling about nothing of importance. Our friends spent that night at our place since they were in no shape to be driving—which can happen when you are having a good time and lose count of how much you've had to drink.

I woke up to the sun streaming into my window and proceeded to the washroom, still wobbly. I stared at my face in the mirror and splashed it with cold water, thinking my present unsteadiness would soon go away. But then I looked closer at my eyes and could see that my pupils appeared different than normal, that the black circles in the middle of my eyes were colossal, as if I had been drinking heavily.

Walking unsteadily back to my room, I got dressed and informed my wife that something was off with me, that the unsteadiness had not gone away since yesterday. Still not thinking too much of it, we both headed to the kitchen, where empty bottles sat on the floor and dirty plates were piled on the table.

When Tucker showed up in the kitchen, we decided to drive five minutes to get coffee and bagels. Getting there was a little strange. I got into his sporty car and we immediately blasted the radio. As we pulled out of the driveway, my head began to spin, but I would not let anything divert my attention from the task of getting something to eat. Even as my body hair began to stand up and droplets of sweat appeared on my forehead, I kept pretending everything was okay so as not to cause a scene. At the drive-through, we placed our order of coffee, bagels, and donuts. I was eating my donut when Tucker suddenly pumped the brakes, making the filling of my donut squirt onto my shirt. Then just as quickly he pressed the gas, causing my heart to crash inside my chest. My face was red, and my eyes were wide open. Finally, he released the gas pedal, but I could see lights in the rearview mirror. We double-checked and yes, it was a police cruiser. Tucker pulled over to the side and the police officer pulled over behind us and approached our car. She then knocked on the window and Tucker was like, "What's the problem, officer?" She replied, "You were speeding and swerving; where are you going in such a hurry?" I chimed in, saying that I had to poop and had told him to speed up. She smiled and let us go, saying to drive slowly and be safe.

Back at the house, we passed around the coffee and toasted bagels, not mentioning to my wife or Lizbeth what had just happened. My symptoms had momentarily disappeared from this excitement, but by the time our friends left for home a few hours later, my unsteadiness was back. Thinking about what this could mean gave me goosebumps; however, I tried not to show it.

I went to sleep that night with darkness in the window and woke up six hours later looking at my clock and realizing it was time for work. But the sunlight through the window looked brighter than usual. Again, I felt like I had been heavily drinking all night. I told my wife, and together we decided I would call in to work and tell them I would be out for the day. I then called our family doctor to explain my issue, and he set up an appointment for that afternoon.

Chapter 2

<u>Doctors Know it All, Right?</u>

We arrived at the doctor's office, and I was given some simple movement tests. I was asked to stand on one leg, which did not happen; I kept losing my balance. I was asked to walk backward, and I somehow managed to accomplish this task, although it took me longer than usual. My doctor sent me straight to a neurologist to dig deeper into what was going on. My hairs stood up and chills came over my body as I entered the neurologist's office. He began by hitting my knee with a rubber hammer to test my reflexes, touching my nose with my eyes closed, and testing my sensation by poking me in different places and having me guess where. I knew something was off when he sent me to the hospital for an MRI of my brain. My heart began to pound rapidly in my chest. The hospital was a few blocks away, and as I approached, I could feel the chills coming again, my heart beating faster and faster the closer I got to the hospital.

I entered the hospital and saw a washroom just inside the doors. Seeing a place that I could be alone, I stepped inside, went to the sink, and turned on the cold water. After splashing my face a few times, I gazed into the mirror and noticed that my face was pale. I turned off the water and dried my face with a paper towel. I looked in the mirror once more, closed my eyes, took a deep breath, and left the washroom. The elevator was right beside the washroom, so I pressed the up button.

I tapped my foot patiently as I waited, but I could feel the goosebumps forming. The elevator door opened, and I pressed the button for the second floor.

The elevator door closed, and the ride up felt like slow motion. It seemed to take 10 minutes to reach the second floor, but it must have been 10 seconds at most. The door opened, and I got out and strolled to the MRI department just a few meters ahead. I approached the secretary and informed her I was there for my brain scan. I was told to take a seat and I'd be called shortly. I sat down, my skin turning red, and grabbed a magazine to read, but before I could open it, I heard my name called. I followed the lady to a gray machine that took up about half the room. In the middle of it was a big tunnel with a place to lay down, and the lady told me to get inside. As soon as my head was resting on the pillow, I was pushed all the way inside the tunnel. The machine began to wind up and I could hear a small object circling my head. It was going faster and getting louder each time it went around, and sometimes it would make a knocking sound. My time in the MRI machine lasted for about 20 minutes. When the scan had finished, the sound gradually slowed until the machine was silent. The technician told me to get up and report back to the neurologist for the results. I did as I was told, my hands wet with sweat.

Once I was in front of the neurologist, my heart once again began to pound and crush against my ribs, but it felt like it was beating in slow motion. The neurologist looked at my MRI, pointing to a chart of the human brain hanging on the brown wall to show me that I had a cyst on my brain stem, just below the brain. He said that they do not operate on that site due to the risk involved. I felt frozen at that moment. I was confused and full of questions, but our meeting was over before I had a chance to ask any. It was only after I left, however, that the reality of the inoperable cyst began to sink in.

The only thing the doctor told me that I understood was that a nurse would visit me daily to check for any changes in my condition. I had no idea how to respond; all I could do was get into my car and start to drive. People were honking at me, but I did not hear. All I could think of was what was going to happen. How would I tell my wife and my parents? This cannot be real, I thought all through the long drive home.

Back home, I repeated what the neurologist had said to my wife. Even then, I did not fully grasp the seriousness of the situation and went about my life, telling myself that this situation wasn't dangerous. I let this positive thought drive out all the doubt in my mind, and as I repeated this mantra to myself over and over, I started to believe it.

Who is Greg Siofer?

Greg Siofer was born in Poland but grew up in the city of Hamilton, Ontario, Canada. He earned his diploma in Web Applications at Mohawk College and helps people in need of balance recovery through online channels. Greg is no stranger to hard times. After a brain cyst operation left him confined to a wheelchair, he struggled through moments of pain and helplessness before finding the determination to make the best of his situation.

Greg has written books that have earned accolades for his unique insight and crafted tales. His accolades, including the Gold Award at Next Generation Indie Book Awards 2022, the Silver Award at Literary Titan 2021, recognition at the New York Book Festival 2021 and the Firebird Book Award 2023.

In his free time, Greg enjoys reading, writing, exercising, and spending time with his daughter and watching Netflix. He also runs a personal blog at *www.iwillbewalking.com* and of course *www.aboutnairb.com* regarding information about Nairb.